"So what are you having?" he asked.

"I don't know. You seem to know what I like."

"What do you like?"

"I'd like for my date to be on time. And in the future, if he's going to be late, I'd like for him to call or text to let me know."

"So you're saying there will be another date. Or should I say, future dates?"

"Let's get through this one first." She smiled at him.

It was easy to be with him, she noted. Some dates were so strained, uncomfortable.

"Fair enough," he said.

"I'll have the fire hot wings," she said.

"Can you handle the fire hot wings?" he asked with a huge grin.

She peeked over the top of the menu. Took note of how handsome he was—dark face, silky, smooth skin. Perfectly trimmed hair and mustache with just a hint of gray. His arms were strong, and his hands were huge. She wondered what it would feel like to be hugged by those arms, but not more than she wondered what the story was behind his sad eyes.

"I can handle a lot." She smiled back at him.

Dear Reader,

Lane Martin is a complicated fellow, sort of like that India Arie song "Complicated Melody"—a melody so complex, it can't be sung on key. That's Lane. Being hurt in love has made him that way. But he's charismatic and easy to fall in love with, despite everything else. He's a truck driver and blue-collar—the total opposite of anything Whitney Talbot is accustomed to. So, she prejudges him, as we often do when we're not accustomed to something.

Sometimes, we only see black and white, and not the gray areas in between. She doesn't quite see or understand the whole of him. And because he has very few qualities on her Man Menu, she almost misses out on the love that could change her life. Not to mention she's dealing with her own fears of love and commitment, which is why these two are made for each other. The chemistry and love between them are undeniable, even though they both spend way too much time denying it.

I hope you fall in love with Lane, and enjoy his and Whitney's story. Writing this book was somewhat effortless, yet intricate all at the same time.

I've thoroughly enjoyed writing the Talbots' story. Because my family is from the Eleuthera Islands, it's like sitting with them and having a great Bahamian meal while researching the beautiful island they call home…and I call *my homeland*. I hope you continue to love the Talbots and make them your favorite family.

Visit my website at monica-richardson.com or email me at Monica@Monica-Richardson.com.

Happy reading!

Monica Richardson

The Unexpected Affair

MONICA RICHARDSON

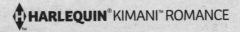

HARLEQUIN® KIMANI™ ROMANCE

Recycling programs
for this product may
not exist in your area.

ISBN-13: 978-0-373-86514-7

The Unexpected Affair

Copyright © 2017 by Monica Richardson

For questions and comments about the quality of this book please contact us at CustomerService@Harlequin.com.

Printed in U.S.A.

Monica Richardson writes adult romances set in Florida and the Caribbean. Under the name Monica McKayhan, she wrote the Indigo Summer young adult series. *Indigo Summer* hit the *Essence* and *Black Issues Book Review* bestseller lists, and the series also received a film option. Monica's YA books have garnered accolades and industry recognition, including several American Library Association (ALA) placements on the Quick Picks for Reluctant Young Adult Readers and the Popular Paperbacks for Young Adults annual lists. She penned her first romance novel, *Tropical Fantasy*, in 2013.

Books by Monica Richardson

Harlequin Kimani Romance

Tropical Fantasy
A Yuletide Affair
An Island Affair
Second Chance Seduction
The Unexpected Affair

Visit the Author Profile page
at Harlequin.com for more titles.

For my granny, Rosa A. Heggie

(November 1927–2008)

She was special in so many ways
and the strongest woman I knew.

My life is rich because of her.

Acknowledgments

To my family and friends—you are my support system.

To my readers—you give me the energy to continue
to write. I'm sure you will enjoy the Talbot family
and get to know them well. This is for you!

To my family in the Bahamas—visiting with you and
talking to you about my history has made the research
and writing of this Talbot series a complete joy.

Chapter 1

Whitney Talbot went over the details of her Man Menu in her head. First and foremost, he needed a college degree. Beyond that, he needed an ample salary and he needed to own at least one piece of real estate. He needed to be tall—at least six feet—dark, handsome. He shouldn't have any children or have been previously married—she didn't need any baby-mama drama. He needed to appreciate the arts and music and love children—because she intended to have at least one, maybe two. He needed to be a conversationalist, because she enjoyed a good conversation.

Her Man Menu was a page long, and she used it loyally. She used it because she and her friends had developed it at the Starbucks just down the street from their college dorm during their Texas A&M. days. They had spent hours pulling it together. It was their bible—their source. They wouldn't be stuck with the wrong man under any circumstances.

After college, Kenya had ended up with Will. Though she spent more time alone because Will traveled 90 percent of the time, she swore that she was happy. He was providing for his family, she always defended him. And though Tasha's husband, Louis, had fathered another woman's child during their marriage, she still swore that he was the perfect man, according to their Man Menu. Yes, he'd made a mistake, but they were repairing their marriage. Marriage took work, she'd say.

All of it terrified Whitney, which was why she had remained the single one in their threesome. She wanted love at the top of her list. Otherwise what was the point? But she wasn't confident that she would find all of the things on her Man Menu plus love. She'd lost faith in that long ago. And as a result, she would date a man just long enough to discover that he was getting too close. Then she'd break things off, regardless of whether he lived up to her Man Menu list of qualities or not. It was easier this way. And though her best girlfriends both proclaimed they were living in romantic bliss, she knew that couldn't be further from the truth.

The dating game had become exhausting and a huge disappointment. Her younger sister, Jasmine, and her older sister, Alyson, had found happiness with good men. She wanted what they had, but men like her brothers-in-law didn't come around that often and surely didn't exist in Texas. She was convinced that they didn't even exist on the planet. And she wasn't taking just any-old-body home to meet her family. Her family was a traditional Bahamian family, and they were certainly a down-to-earth bunch. But their impression of her was that she'd gone away and done well for herself—and she needed to live up to that image. If she took a man home, he needed to be perfect and their connection needed to be real. Her family would see right through her. She was the middle girl and didn't need nearly as much attention as her other sisters, but she needed a man who loved her. And she needed to love him, for that matter.

She'd gone to college in Texas and landed a teaching position at a local elementary school in Dallas. She wasn't crazy about Texas but vowed never to return to the Caribbean for any length of time. She needed her independence, and her family wouldn't allow that if she moved back home. They would be all up in her business, running her life. She had almost entertained the thought of it when she and her siblings had inherited three historical properties from their grandparents. Her family had since transformed the properties into beautiful B and Bs along the Bahamian coast. Though she hadn't been there during the renovation, her siblings had been instrumental in making the Grove the extraordinary property that it was. It had quickly become one of the most sought-after properties on Harbour Island.

She'd promised her family that once the property was up and running, she'd return home after the school year ended and help out with the family business. Unfortunately, returning never happened and she hoped they wouldn't bring it up. After the Grove was fully staffed, she figured there was no need for her services, and she was fine with that.

Her older brother Edward had recently remarried his ex-wife, Savannah. They'd fallen in love all over again—or was it that they'd never fallen out of love? Whichever the case, they were throwing a huge soiree in the Caribbean at the family's property to celebrate their nuptials. The entire family was expected to be there, and she was no exception. It seemed that every time she turned around, the Talbot family was celebrating something and expecting her to hop on a plane and traipse to the islands as though they were just around the corner. She loved her family and loved spending time with them, but she was tired of returning home for these parties and celebrations and she was the only one without a man. So before she headed off to the Bahamas for another blessed event, she was determined to find that perfect someone to accommodate her.

Her best friend, Kenya, claimed to have the perfect guy for her.

"He has everything on the menu, girl!" Kenya squealed. "I swear."

"Sounds too good to be true," said a doubtful Whitney.

"Okay, maybe not every single thing, but most stuff," Kenya assured her. "You have to be a little flexible or you're going to be alone for the rest of your life! And you have to stop running guys away when they get too close. Thomas was perfect for you, but you…"

"I don't mind being alone, Kenya. I'll die alone before I settle."

"Well, you need somebody to take home to the Caribbean, right?"

"Right," Whitney resolved. "I guess we don't have to get married or anything. I just want him to impress my father, who is a retired physician, and my mother, who was an educator—in her other life."

"First of all, I've met both of your parents. They're sweet as pie…not one bit judgmental. I think they just want the best for you—whatever makes you happy," said Kenya. "Which reminds me. Did you tell them how miserable you are teaching little kindergartners?"

Whitney loved her teaching career. Loved making a difference in the lives of her children. She wasn't miserable and certainly had no plans of leaving her day job. Her mother would be crushed if she even thought she was leaving the teaching realm. After all, Beverly Talbot lived her teaching career vicariously through Whitney, and she wouldn't let her mother down. However, she *had* found that songwriting made her heart soar. She'd been writing on the side and it actually made a good supplement to her teacher's income, and it gave her a creative outlet. And when someone had actually performed one of her original pieces at Kenya's birthday party, she'd actually entertained the idea of doing it full-time. That is, until her friend Tasha shot the idea down and made her feel ridiculous for even considering it. Needless to say, her good sense had kicked in and knocked her back into reality. Besides not wanting to disappoint her mother, she would never squander her education. Her father had worked too hard to put her and her siblings through college. Not to mention, she loved her children.

"I'm not miserable teaching, and I haven't told them anything. In fact, I haven't decided what my career plans are. I'm just taking it a day at a time."

"You'll figure it out, Whit. You always do." Kenya was always her encourager. "Anyway, Will and I will meet you at the Cheesecake Factory at six. His friend Jason will be there, too. He won't have much time, because he has another commitment after dinner. But he desperately wants to meet you. He's educated, a business owner, fine as hell…"

"Is he tall?"

"He's not quite six feet, but he owns a home in Mansfield and some commercial property, too." Kenya skirted right past the issue of his height. "He has a house on the beach in Galveston."

"Okay, fine," Whitney resolved. She hated blind dates but didn't want to disappoint Kenya.

"Be on time, Whitney," warned Kenya. "He's a busy man and has another commitment."

"Fine."

Whitney had a commitment of her own. She'd just purchased a lot in the new housing development in Cedar Hill, near Joe Pool Lake. Her first taste of home-ownership and she was beyond excited. She'd long outgrown her Dallas condo and was tired of the hustle and bustle of Dallas traffic. She was having her dream home built and couldn't wait to do her daily drive-by to see how things were coming along. She just wanted a peek and hoped she could make it to the new development and then back to Sundance Square in downtown Fort Worth for her blind date with the good friend of Kenya's fiancé's. She hoped that Dallas traffic would be milder than usual.

As she pulled her Nissan into the development, she smiled when she saw the cement truck backing into one of the lots. They were building more homes in her popular neighborhood. She drove to the cul-de-sac at the end of the block, turned around and came back. Kenya sent her a text and she looked down—for a split second—to read it, and when she looked up, she realized that the cement truck was now moving forward and not backward. She'd already slammed into the side of it before she knew it.

"Dammit!" she exclaimed as the phone hit the floor. She put the vehicle in Park and stepped out of the car. She smoothed her dress over her hips.

The driver hopped down from the truck, a frown on his face. "Lady, what were you doing?"

He wore an orange-and-silver reflective safety vest, but all Whitney saw was the tight gray T-shirt underneath that hugged his biceps. With a hard hat on his head, he pulled the dark shades from his eyes and peered at her.

"I'm so sorry. I just looked down for a split second," she said. "When I looked up, there you were."

"What are you even doing here? This is no place for you to be driving around."

"I'm here because right over there is my house—my lot!" She pointed at the space across the street where the foundation of a home had just begun to be built. "I have every right to be here."

"You should watch where you're going." He pulled his cell phone out of his pocket, called his company to explain the details of the incident. She gave an apologetic smile to the other workers who had gathered at the scene. They weren't at all happy with having their workday interrupted. The ordeal seemed to last longer than she'd hoped.

She hated to ask but knew that she had another commitment. "Can we speed this along? I really have somewhere else I need to be," she stated as they awaited the arrival of the local police.

"You're serious." A slight smile danced in the corner of his mouth.

"Yes, I'm serious."

"You should've thought about your other commitment before you hit my truck," he said. "There's a process to this."

She rolled her eyes at him, pulled her cell phone out,

called Kenya and explained that she wouldn't make it for her blind date.

"Blind date, huh?" he asked after she hung up.

"Were you eavesdropping on my conversation?"

"I couldn't help it. You weren't exactly whispering."

Mr. Cement-Truck-Driver was quickly getting under her skin, but she tried to remain calm.

"It's rude to listen in on people's conversations. And even more rude to put your two cents in."

"I didn't know people actually did blind dates anymore."

"Well, they do," she said.

"I see."

She ignored him and began to engage in text messaging with Kenya until the officer arrived. The officer jotted down each of their contact information, gave them each a copy and then disappeared in his patrol car. She glanced at her copy. Lane Martin was his name. She crumpled the paper and stuck it into her purse. Headed for her car.

"Why do you need a blind date, anyway?" he asked. "You shouldn't have any trouble finding a man."

"For your information, I don't have trouble finding a man," she stated, "not that I'm looking."

A slight smile danced in the corner of his mouth again. He seemed to enjoy getting under her skin. "I'm sorry about your car."

"My insurance will be through the roof, if they don't cancel me."

"Yeah, I know what you mean. Insurance companies are crooks anyway."

She stood there, when she should've been moving toward her car. She was mesmerized by him. Couldn't take her eyes off his chest. He was tall, a big strong guy. Football-player strong, she thought.

"I'm Lane. Sorry we got off to a bad start." He held his hand out to her.

"Whitney." She took his strong hand in hers. She appreciated the ruggedness of it. It wasn't soft, and his nails weren't manicured, but they were decent—clean and trimmed.

"That accent. Jamaican?" he asked.

"Bahamian."

"It's nice."

"Thank you," she said. She got that all the time. People loved her Caribbean accent.

"So that's going to be your new home, huh?" he asked, pointing at the lot across the street.

"Yes."

"Congratulations." He smiled genuinely. "I poured the concrete over there, too."

"Thank you, I guess," she said, looking at her watch. "I really have to go."

"Oh, that's right." There was that beautifully sly grin again. "Blind date."

The truth was, she'd already missed her blind date, and she wasn't even mad about it. In fact, she felt somewhat relieved. She hadn't been too keen on meeting yet another guy she wouldn't be the least bit attracted to. She would only go through the motions and hope that she'd find something about him that she could tolerate.

"Good day, Lane," she said. "It was a pleasure meeting you."

She was grateful for the dress she'd chosen that day. The one that hugged her ample hips in just the right places. She put an extra swing in them as she made her way back to her Nissan.

"Pleasure was all mine," she heard him say. No doubt he was watching the rhythm of her hips.

As she sank into the driver's seat of her car, she exhaled. She glanced at Lane. Just as she'd suspected, he was, in fact, watching—his arms folded across his chest as he leaned against his truck. She was nervous, and just making it to her car had been a challenge. Her heart pounded. Why was she behaving this way? This guy most likely met very few of the requirements on her Man Menu. She started her car, turned up the volume on the Jill Scott tune that amplified through her speakers. Gave him a slight wave as she pulled away.

He was not her type. She was sure of it.

Chapter 2

Lane Martin needed another incident like he needed a hole in his head. He'd just been written up for another incident a month prior. He'd been with the company for almost twenty years but the new company supervisor had it in for him. He didn't need any more trouble. His job was his pride and joy. He wasn't working in the field of his degree. Instead he'd chosen to work with his hands, rather than selling out for a white-collar position in corporate America. Though he'd invested well, he didn't believe in splurging on unnecessary things. He owned a modest ranch-style brick home on the outskirts of Mesquite, Texas, and drove a regular old pickup—a ten-year-old Ford F-150. He hadn't bought a new vehicle since his divorce. He knew that he would have to send his son to college one day, although he still had several years before Lane Jr. even thought about college.

Even at the age of thirteen Lane Jr. was already an

impressive athlete. Lane had been an impressive athlete, as well. He'd attended Mizzou on a football scholarship and had been a running back. At one time, he had hopes of being picked up by the Dallas Cowboys, but a fatal car wreck had robbed him of those dreams. His life had changed the night that he and his older brother Tye had been celebrating a football victory. Tye insisted on driving them home, although they'd each had one too many drinks. Neither of them was awake when they plowed into the rear end of an 18-wheeler. Tye didn't survive the crash, and sometimes Lane thought that he hadn't either. His life came to a screeching halt that night. He blamed himself for the accident. If only he'd convinced Tye not to drive, he would still be alive. From that night on, Lane had no desire to ever play football again.

He jumped into a marriage to try to mask the pain of losing his brother but failed miserably as a young husband. By the time he realized that his marriage was over, it was too late—his wife was leaving him. He packed his things into his car, kissed his toddler son goodbye and went out to find his way in the world. He was determined to be better at fatherhood than he had been at marriage, and so far he was batting a thousand. Alongside having a career that he was proud of, making a nice salary and owning a nice home in a small Texas town, being a father was right there at the top of his greatest-achievements list.

Grief, fear and failure had robbed him of ever finding love again. However, after exchanging information with the beautiful stranger who had run into his cement truck, he had to admit, she was attractive. He remembered how she kept going on and on about having to report the accident to her insurance company and the risk of higher premiums—or worse, cancellation. He thought maybe he could fix things for her. That was what he was—a fixer. Always fixing others' problems. Yet his problems had gone unsolved.

He kicked his boots off at the door and opened each piece of mail that he'd gathered from the box. He plopped down on the sofa in his family room, rested his head against the back of it. Working long hours usually left him exhausted. He grabbed the remote control and tuned the television to ESPN, caught the commentary before the playoff game was to begin. Watching sports after a hard day's work was usually the highlight of his day. Except for today. The highlight today had been the beautiful stranger who had rammed her car into his cement truck. He hadn't been able to get her out of his head since the moment he'd laid eyes on her.

He made his way into the kitchen and checked the chicken that he'd placed in the slow cooker that morning before work. He tasted a piece and closed his eyes. It was perfectly seasoned and tender. Over the years, he'd become a great cook. Bachelorhood had taught him self-sufficiency and he'd mastered it. He grabbed a bottle of beer from the refrigerator and made his way into the bathroom for a long, hot shower.

He dried his hair and then wrapped the towel around his waist. He put on a pair of basketball shorts and pulled an old Mizzou T-shirt over his head. He wasn't startled when he heard the doorbell ring. It wasn't unusual for his best friend, Melvin, to show up unannounced, and especially on the night of a playoff game. Before Lane could answer the door, Melvin was already inside.

"It's game time!" Melvin yelled, a baseball cap turned backward on his head and a Cavaliers jersey barely covering his belly.

"You smelled the food cooking," said Lane.

"Now that you mention it—" Melvin raised his eyebrows "—what are we eating?"

"*We* aren't eating anything," said Lane with a grin.

Melvin usually made himself right at home. And today was no different as he reached into the refrigerator and grabbed himself a beer. "Last beer, bro," said Melvin, raising it into the air.

"Well, maybe you should run on down to the store and grab *us* another six-pack."

"At halftime, bro," Melvin promised as he plopped down in the chair in front of the television.

Lane knew that he wouldn't be making the beer run. He never did. "I'm holding you to it."

"Halftime. I promise," said Melvin. "How long before dinner?"

Lane laughed at his best friend, who had been his college roommate and his teammate on the football field. Melvin knew him better than anyone—had been with him through all of the highs and lows of his life: his marriage to Helena, his divorce from Helena, the death of his brother. He'd been his rock, and often his sounding board. Melvin was family. They'd grown up in Saint Louis together. And after Lane had moved to Texas and gotten settled, Melvin soon followed. Slept on his couch for a few months until he'd finally landed a job and his own place.

Lane described his day to Melvin—told him about the woman crashing into his cement truck. "She was concerned about filing a claim with her insurance," said Lane.

"Was it a bad dent?"

"Not too bad. Nothing you can't handle."

In addition to owning his own accounting firm,

Melvin also tinkered with old cars. He owned a body shop in South Dallas where he transformed old cars into new ones. He also worked with insurance companies to repair damaged cars.

"Have her bring it over to the shop, and I'll knock it out for her."

"Really?"

"Of course," said Melvin. "Why are you so concerned about it, anyway?"

"She was a nice lady. Just trying to help her out."

"Mmm-hmm. I see," said Melvin. "She cute?"

"She's not bad on the eyes."

Melvin had been slouching in the chair. He sat straight up. "You like her."

It was a statement, not a question.

"I don't even know her, bro. I'm just trying to help her out."

"Right," said Melvin as he made his way to the kitchen to fix himself a plate. "You can do something for me, too."

"What?"

"Tyler needs a job," said Melvin. "You know my nephew Tyler. He's moving in with me for a few months. Needs a new start. Getting into all kinds of trouble in Saint Louis. His daddy thinks he'll do much better here in Texas. Maybe you can get him on down there at the plant."

"Does he have any experience?"

"Fast food. But he's smart. He'll catch on fast."

"I don't know, man," said Lane. He'd been burned too many times before trying to help people out. Situations like this ruined relationships. "Youngsters aren't dependable."

"He'll be dependable. I'll make sure of it."

Lane shook his head. He didn't like the idea of putting his job on the line for people, but he knew Tyler. And he knew how it was growing up in Saint Louis and running with the wrong crowd. "Have him come down and see me on Monday. I'll see what I can do."

"He'll do good, man. I promise."

"He'd better."

Lane disappeared into his bedroom for privacy, shut the door. Pulled the folded piece of paper from the pocket of his work pants, unfolded it and searched for Whitney's phone number. She answered on the second ring.

"Hello."

"Hey," he said nervously. "It's Lane Martin. You know, from the accident today."

"Oh, hello."

"I'm sorry to call so late. But…" he paused "…I just wanted to tell you, I have a friend who owes me a favor and can knock that dent right out of your bumper. You can take your car over there tomorrow. That way you won't have to report it to your insurance company."

"Really?" she asked. "Why would you do that?"

"Because I'm a nice guy," he said with a smile in his voice. "And my best friend owns a body shop."

"Okay," she said cheerfully. "I appreciate it."

"No problem."

"Text me the address of the shop."

"Okay, I will. As soon as we hang up."

"Cavs up by two!" Melvin yelled from the other room. "Lane, get your ass in here!"

Whitney giggled. "Sounds like you need to go."

"Sounds like I do."

"Thank you again," said Whitney.

"No problem. Have a good night," said Lane. "And I'll text the information right away."

"Great."

She hung up.

He sat there on the edge of the bed for a moment, a subtle smile in the corner of his mouth. He typed the address to Melvin's shop into a text message, hit the send key and then made his way back to the game.

Chapter 3

Whitney glanced at the text message. She was grateful for the gesture, Lane arranging to have her car repaired. She shut her phone case and walked over to the baby grand piano that rested in her living room. She loved her piano, though it crowded her space, which was another reason she was having a house built. She needed the extra space for her baby.

She'd played the piano since the age of twelve and had mastered it. Music was her lifeline. She was from a musical family—her grandfather and father were both musicians. So her love for music made sense. In addition to playing, she wrote songs. She'd written a few pieces and sold them. Songwriting had brought about a nice supplement to her teaching income. She'd even entertained the thought that if she wrote full-time, she could probably make her current teaching salary or more. But the fear of not having a secure income always trumped her love for writing.

Whitney started a bubble bath and lit a candle. She'd gone to the gym, and a bath after a workout always soothed her aching muscles. She sipped on a glass of red wine to wash down the chicken breast and brown rice that she'd prepared for dinner. She peeled sweaty clothes from her body, pulled her hair up into a bun and stepped into the bathtub. She needed to steal a few moments to pamper herself before settling in for the night.

When she slipped into bed, sleep came quickly. She'd fallen asleep long before nine thirty and with the television blaring with Don Lemon's commentary on CNN. It seemed that morning always came abruptly.

Whitney moseyed over to the door, opened it. The bell rang and fifteen kindergartners rushed from their chairs and headed toward the door.

"Excuse me!" exclaimed Whitney. "I don't remember dismissing anyone."

The children slowly made their way back to their respective seats, waited patiently for their teacher to give them permission to move.

"Now you may form a single-file line in front of me. Bus riders first."

The children formed a line in front of the door, and Whitney escorted them out of the classroom, through the hallway of their elementary school, past the office and out the side door where the buses waited for them to get on board. She ushered all of the children to the correct school buses or to their parents' cars. After seeing that all the children made it to their modes of transportation, Whitney made her way back to her classroom.

She sat at her desk and graded a few papers, turned on her laptop and checked her email. This was her quiet time. She loved her children but looked forward to those quiet moments when they all went home. After responding to emails from parents and shutting down her computer, she tidied the classroom a bit. Placed crayons and bottles of glue into cubbyholes and threw trash away.

She checked her watch. She had just enough time to make her appointment at the body shop. Lane's friend Melvin had promised to make her car look like new. She looked forward to it and appreciated Lane for even suggesting it. She grabbed her purse from the locked bottom drawer of her desk, pulled her keys out. She shut off the lights in her classroom on her way out the door. Her cell phone buzzed. Kenya.

"Hey, girl," she answered.

"I need a drink," said Kenya. "Meet me at Duffy's."

"Can't. I have an appointment."

"Oh, Whit! Are you going to make me drink alone?" Kenya whined.

"Why do you need a drink so badly?"

"Will's mother is in town. You know she gives me hives. I can't do anything right with her!" said Kenya.

"Oh, no! Not his mama."

"She's already started. Now she's trying to plan the wedding. I don't mind her input, but damn, this is my wedding," said Kenya. "She's added like twenty extra people to the guest list."

"No!"

"Twenty extra mouths to feed!"

"What does Will say?"

"That's just my mom, babe." Kenya's voice was in a baritone as she mocked her fiancé. "You know how she is."

Whitney laughed. "Sorry."

"This is so not funny, Whit. I'm going crazy!" Kenya exhaled. "She wants to look for alternate choices for the rehearsal dinner, and now she's asking why the brides-maids' dresses have to be so provocative."

"Did she specifically say bridesmaids' dresses, or did she mention my maid-of-honor dress, too?" Whitney laughed.

"Whit!"

"You do need a drink," said Whitney. "Meet me at the body shop and we can find somewhere to go from there."

"Thank you. Damn, girl."

"I'll text you the address."

Whitney bid the custodian a good night with a nod. He gave her a wide grin, and had she not been on the phone, he'd have struck up a long conversation about his ailing mother. Once Whitney revealed to him that she was from the Bahamas islands, he always went on and on about his Caribbean roots. She walked out the door quickly and to her car.

She waited for Melvin to appear in the customer waiting area after the receptionist called for him. He was not at all what she'd expected, actually the opposite of the image she had in her head—he was clean shaven, tall and handsome. Not at all a body-shop type of guy. She shook his hand.

"Good to meet you," she said.

"Pleasure's mine." His smile was handsome. "Let's take a look at that dent."

He followed her outside to her car.

"Here it is." She pointed at her vehicle.

"Ouch," he said. "But it's not so bad. Won't take me long to knock that out."

"Good. I appreciate it."

"No problem. Lane is my best friend," he told her. "And he insisted that I take good care of you."

"Did he, now?"

"Yes, but he didn't mention that you were so beautiful and had a sexy accent. Where are you from?"

"Bahamas."

"Nice," said Melvin. "Now, if you'll just have a seat in the customer waiting area, I'll get you squared away."

"Actually, my girlfriend just pulled up. We're going to run out for a bit, and I'll just come back in a little while."

Melvin squinted to get a better look at Kenya as she pulled into the parking lot. "She look like you?" He smiled.

"She's engaged." Whitney smiled and began to walk out of the shop.

"Engaged, but not married, right?" he called as she walked away.

"They're just about there." Whitney laughed, giving Melvin a wave as she exited. She hopped into the passenger's seat of Kenya's sedan.

Kenya lowered the volume on the Rihanna song she was blasting. "Who's the nosy guy?"

"Melvin." Whitney wrapped the seat belt around her. "Lane's friend."

"Oh, Lane." Kenya grinned. "Now you're on a first-name basis."

"What? His name is Lane. You want me to keep calling him *the guy whose truck I plunged into*?"

"I guess not." Kenya gave her a side-eye. "Now, where around here can we go for that drink? I don't know anything about this neighborhood."

"Right," said Whitney, pulling her cell phone out of her purse. "I'll just check Yelp."

"Okay."

"It says there's a bar just around the corner. They have great reviews and even have a happy hour," said Whitney. "Make a left here at the corner."

They stepped into the quaint bar, snagged a small table in the corner of the dimly lit room. Soulful music played casually, and some people swayed to it, while others engaged in loud conversations. Whitney ordered her signature rum and pineapple juice, while Kenya sipped on a glass of Merlot.

"Can we have an order of the hot wings, too?" Whitney asked the half-naked server.

"Surc," said the young woman. "You want mild or hot?"

"What do you think?" she asked Kenya.

"I'm not eating any hot wings. Girl, I've got to fit all of this into that wedding dress in a few weeks."

Kenya was always watching her weight. Always on some diet or taking a supplement for this or that. And since getting engaged, she'd been on a mission to maintain her weight at her current size because she was not buying another dress.

"I'll take the hot ones," said Whitney, and as soon as the server walked away, she leaned toward Kenya to talk over the music. "A few hot wings never hurt anybody."

"I'm not like you, with your perfect figure that you never have to work for!"

"Oh, I work for it. But I cheat sometimes," said Whitney. "I hit the gym, too."

"When, Whit?" asked Kenya. "When was the last time you were committed to a workout?"

"Last night."

"But before that, how long?"

"It had been…" Whitney thought for a moment, took a sip of her drink. "Okay, it had been a while. But I'm back now. I'm sore right now, but I'm back."

"Why do you bother?" asked Kenya. "Look at you. You've got it in all the right places."

Whitney's five-foot-four physique was coveted by many. Her 152 pounds seemed to fall in all the right places. In her mind, though, she needed work. She needed her butt lifted and her stomach flatter.

"So do you. You just need to tone a bit," said Whitney. She knew that weight had been a long-standing and touchy subject for Kenya, so she changed the subject. "I found the perfect shoes for my dress."

"Really? Where?"

"DSW." Whitney pulled her cell phone out, sorted through her photos and showed Kenya. "Look at these beauties."

"Oh, they are beautiful!" Kenya grabbed the phone. "I need to send this to all of the bridesmaids."

Whitney snatched her phone back. Her Bahamian accent was stronger at times. "No, honey. I'm the maid of honor. My dress *and* shoes will be different."

"You're right," Kenya resolved. "It's just that these women are dragging their feet. I don't even think that Tasha has gone to get fitted for her dress!"

"She will." Whitney laughed. "You know she's late for everything. She'll be late for her own funeral."

"Why can't she ever be on time?" Kenya took a sip of her wine and made room on the table for the piping-hot wings that the server placed on the table. "Thanks, honey. Can we get some extra napkins, please?"

The server walked away, but not before rolling her eyes at Kenya.

"Did she just roll her damn eyes at me?" Kenya asked.

Whitney chuckled. "I think she did."

"See, that's why I don't come over here."

"It's okay." Whitney was already tearing into a hot wing and licking sauce from her fingertips. "Some of the best places have the worst customer service. Try these wings, girl. You'll forget all about what's-her-name."

"I'm going to pretend I didn't see it." Kenya grabbed a wing, her pinkie finger in the air.

Whitney shook her head and grabbed another wing.

Just as they pulled up at the body shop, Melvin was pulling Whitney's car out of the bay.

"You're all set." He stepped out of the car, grinned and dangled the keys in the air.

"Thank you." Whitney gave him a smile and grabbed her keys. She took a long look at her bumper. It was like new. "Looks good!"

"Damn right!" he boasted. "Now, tell my friend Lane that I took good care of you."

"I certainly will." She walked around to the side of her car. Melvin opened the door for her and she sank into the driver's seat. "Thank you."

"My pleasure." He slammed her door shut.

She drove off, found a track on her playlist and smiled as the music resonated through the car.

Chapter 4

Lane relaxed on the sofa and flipped back and forth between two football games. Why they had to air them at the same time was beyond him. He had bets riding on both of them. He wasn't a gambler in the traditional sense, he'd convinced himself. He just dabbled a bit. He didn't need the money. In fact, he'd made a nice salary driving his cement truck for the past seventeen years. Betting on sports was just a pastime. He could quit at any time.

He yelled at the television, a plate of food on the coffee table in front of him. He sipped on a cold bottle of Budweiser, leaned back on the pillow and pushed the comforter aside. The sofa doubled as a bed for him because that's where he slept most nights. It had been weeks since he'd slept in his bed. He worked insane hours, and usually he'd fall asleep in front of the television before the last quarter of any game. He was the epitome of a bachelor, and his relationships had struggled in the past. His long hours left minimal time for dating.

Besides working long hours, he hadn't found a woman worth the work of dating long-term. He usually found something wrong with her. Too clingy, too self-centered, too fat, too skinny, low self-esteem—all were reasons to break things off before anyone got serious. His divorce had left him gun-shy, and he wasn't sure that he'd let anyone else in after that. Love was painful, and he didn't have time to be hurt again.

His phone buzzed and he looked at the text message.

Just left Melvin's shop. Thanks for everything!

"Whitney," he whispered. A smile swept across his face, and he couldn't wipe it away.

He replied, Yrr welcome.

He wanted to say more but didn't want to give her the wrong impression. Didn't want her to think that he was interested in anything more than making sure her car was taken care of. He placed the phone on the coffee table and stuffed a forkful of green beans into his mouth.

I hope you have a nice night, she texted back.

You too, he replied, and then waited for the notification that she had texted him again.

He waited. Grabbed the phone and typed, Are you free Friday night?

What was he doing? Friday night was his night to fall asleep in front of the television again. He didn't need to make appointments that he had no intentions of keeping. He hit the send key anyway.

Free for what? she asked.

Idk. Dinner?

"I don't know?" he whispered. "Dammit!"

He didn't even have a game plan. He'd approached her without a plan. And on top of that, he wasn't even sure if he really wanted to take her out. It was just something that had slipped out, an impulsive act on his part.

Sure, she texted.

Had she said yes? He sat up straight on the sofa, stuck his chest out. He was cocky now.

Cool, he typed.

Where would he take her? She was undoubtedly a wine-sipping fancy-dinner-spot type of woman. He was a sports-bar type of guy. That was a good enough reason not to follow through with this crazy idea. He leaned against the back of the sofa, considered how he could get out of this date that he'd just made on impulse. How had he even gotten here? They were as different as night and day. And he wasn't up for anyone trying to change him. Nope. He'd been there, done that with the last woman, Erica. She'd tried her best to change him. Buying him these corny outfits and insisting that he wear them to the cocktail parties and office dinners that he'd been forced to tag along on. She hated when he watched the game or hung out with the guys from work. Wanted him to spend every waking hour with her. He was relieved when she finally disappeared from his life.

I know a nice sports bar in the Arts District. The Cowboys are playing that night. Not that I'm a fan of the Cowboys, but I enjoy a good football game, she texted.

He smiled when he read the text. "Damn," he whispered.

Well, who are you a fan of? he asked.

Broncos. I don't know why. I grew up watching soccer myself, but I just like the team. You?

Kansas City Chiefs. After my hometown, Saint Louis, lost the Rams to LA, I went with the next best team.

The Chiefs? The next best?

He laughed aloud and then dialed her phone number. Forget the texting. He needed to set her straight! She was laughing on the other end of the phone.

"You think that's funny, huh?" he asked.

"Did I push your buttons?" she asked, still laughing.

"What do you have against the Chiefs?"

"I'm not saying that they're crap overall. Their season is pretty good this year."

"They're doing great this season!"

"You're right. And they do have Andy Reid."

"What you know about football?"

"I know a lot," she said. "Now, are we meeting at the sports bar on Friday night or what?"

"Send me the info and I'll meet you there," he said. He tried to remain calm. Friday wouldn't get here soon enough, he thought.

"Good!" she exclaimed. "I'll see you then."

"Okay."

"I'd love to talk to you more about the Chiefs, but I have an early morning with twelve kindergartners. I need my beauty sleep."

"I wouldn't want to interrupt your beauty sleep. It seems to be working pretty good." He chuckled.

"I'll see you on Friday." Her voice smiled.

"Have a good night."

"You, too."

He held the phone long after she'd hung up. He took his plate into the kitchen and washed the few dishes that were in the sink. He grabbed another beer from the fridge and decided that he'd turn in for the night, as well. Three o'clock in the morning usually came knocking a lot sooner than he was ever ready for.

Lane pulled his Ford F-150 into the parking lot. Sat there for a moment and gathered his thoughts. It was early, and though he'd done these hours for many years, he still needed a moment each morning. He listened to the ending of the song on his playlist before finally shutting the engine off. Made his way across the gravel to the office and punched the time clock. He made his way over to his cement truck, hopped into the driver's seat and started the engine. He smiled at the rumble of it. He hopped out and then did an inspection of his truck. Priscilla, he called her. He and Priscilla had been together for many years. He'd been with Priscilla longer than his ex-wife.

When he heard the sound of a notification on his phone, he pulled it out of his pocket.

Don't forget about LJ's game, the text read.

Helena had a bad habit of reminding him of things he already knew. Two games. He'd had to work late a couple of times and missed two games, and she hadn't let him forget it.

I'll be there, he typed.

And don't forget he needs new sneakers, she added.

Got them already.

He was becoming more irritated by the moment. He didn't need her reminding him of things he already knew. He wasn't her husband anymore. In fact, she had new a husband now. She needed to tend to what's-his-name and stay out of his affairs with his son. He and LJ had things under control. They talked every afternoon when he got out of school. LJ kept his father abreast of his game schedule, his grades and everything that was important to him. He'd even asked for advice about girls on occasion—*a rare occasion.*

LJ was somewhat shy, laid-back. Unlike his father at that age, who was a social butterfly. He'd had no problems talking to girls in high school, and certainly not in college. Being a star running back at both schools, he was popular. There was no need for him to chase, because girls flocked to him. And he basked in the glory of it—until that one girl captured his heart. The one he married. The one who broke his heart. They were supposed to live happily ever after, but his happily-ever-after quickly changed when she walked out of his life, their son in tow. He swore that no one would ever get the chance to do that to him again. Ever.

He placed the hard hat on his head and secured his reflective safety vest around his torso. He turned up the volume on the radio—listened to the antics of the disc jockeys on the hip-hop station, K104. He slowly pulled the cement truck out of the parking lot and headed for his first job of the day. Tried not to think about Whitney, but he couldn't help it. She was already creeping into his thoughts, uninvited.

Chapter 5

She sat on the rooftop patio, at the high-top table, and sipped on a glass of water. She checked her watch. It was already seven fifteen. They'd agreed to meet at seven, and she was there at six forty-five. She was always prompt and expected nothing less from her suitors. Promptness was an item on her Man Menu. It was right up there with cleanliness. In the past, she'd have walked out and never answered her phone again. But something made her sit there and wait, even as seven thirty flashed across the big-screen television where the Cowboys had just scored a field goal.

"Can I get you something else to drink, ma'am?" asked the blond-haired server.

"She'll have a Heineken," said the male voice behind her, "and one for me, too."

She wanted to tell him about his tardiness. Had already rehearsed the speech in her head, but when she looked at his beautiful chocolate face and he flashed that beautiful smile, everything she thought she wanted to say dissipated. He cleaned up well, and the jeans and black shirt were a nice change from his work attire. Lane kissed her cheek and took a seat across from her at the table.

"What makes you think I wanted a beer?"

"It's a sports bar. The game is on…" He grinned. "I can order you something else if you'd like."

"What makes you think I wanted you to order for me at all?" She almost smiled. "I'm fully capable of ordering for myself."

"I couldn't tell. When I walked in, you were sipping on a glass of water." He grabbed a menu and began to look it over.

"You were late," she mentioned.

"I'm sorry. My last job lasted a little later than expected. I had to rush home, shower and change."

"No text to say 'I'm running late'?" she asked.

"I'm so sorry. That was totally inconsiderate of me," he said. "Forgive me?"

She grabbed a menu and held it up to her face. "This time," she said.

"Thank you."

The server placed a beer in front of each of them. She looked at the green bottle and watched as Lane poured his into the chilled mug. She wasn't a beer drinker but liked the idea of trying something new. She poured hers into the mug and took a sip. It wasn't as bad as she'd anticipated.

"So what are you having?" he asked.

"I don't know. You seem to know what I like."

"What do you like?"

"I'd like for my date to be on time. And in the future, if he's going to be late, I'd like for him to call or text and let me know."

"So you're saying there will be another date. Or should I say, future dates."

"Let's get through this one first." She smiled at him.

He was easy to be with, she noted. Some dates were so strained, uncomfortable.

"Fair enough," he said.

"I'll have the fire hot wings," she said.

"Can you handle the fire hot wings?" he asked with a grin.

She peeked over the top of the menu. Took note of how handsome he was—dark face, silky smooth skin, perfectly trimmed hair and mustache with just a hint of gray. His arms were strong, and his hands were huge. She wondered what it would feel like to be hugged by those arms, but more than that she wondered what the story was behind those sad eyes.

"I can handle a lot," she flirted.

"Really?"

"Yes, really." She smiled.

"I know you teach kindergarten for a living, but what do you do for fun?" he asked.

"I sing, play the piano and write music."

"Really?" He was surprised. "Let me hear something."

"No!" She smiled.

"Why not? It's just me and you," he encouraged.

"Not the time or place."

"Chicken."

"I guess I am," she said. She felt comfortable with him, but not comfortable enough to sing. Not just yet.

"Fine. One day."

"One day."

"You're beautiful." He watched her, and even when she looked away, he didn't break the stare.

"Thank you," she said while looking at the television.

"Your accent is sexy," he said. "I bet you get that all the time, though."

"I get it quite a bit."

"So what do you do when you're not teaching children or singing?"

"Either hanging with my girls or watching Netflix—*alone.* Not Netflix and chill," she said.

He laughed. "Okay."

"What about you? When you're not driving a cement truck, what are you doing?" she asked.

"I'm at my son's football games, yelling at the ref to call the right plays. I've been banned from the field twice." He laughed.

"Wow! No self-control."

"I have self-control. I just like to get my point across."

"By getting thrown from the field," she said sarcastically. "Yeah, that will definitely get your point across."

"You've been teaching little people too long." He pointed a finger her way.

She laughed. "We need to exercise self-control."

She pointed a finger at him. He unexpectedly grabbed her small hand, stroked in between her fingers. Rubbed the ring finger on her left hand.

"No shadow where a ring should be."

She pulled her hand away. "What? I'm not married!"

"You can't be too careful with these women out here." He laughed. "They pretend to be single, when they're really married."

"What type of women are you running into?"

"All types. It's why I've been single for so long. I don't trust anyone."

"That's a hard way to live."

"You always get taken for a ride in this game," he stated. "No feelings. No trust. It's the only way to be."

"When was your last serious relationship?"

"My marriage. Been divorced five years. Since my son was five years old."

"I'm sorry."

"Why are you sorry? I'm not. She got what she wanted. She wanted out," he said. "My only regret is that I can't live in the same home with my son. But it's okay. I see him often, and we talk every day."

"That's good."

"We were young, fresh out of college."

She mentally checked his education off on her Man Menu. He was a college graduate, and that was definitely a plus.

"What college did you graduate from?"

"Mizzou."

"Tigers, huh?"

"All day."

"What's your degree in?" she asked.

"Computer science." He took a sip of his beer.

"Why aren't you working in your degree, for some major software company? I bet there are millions of them in Dallas."

"Because I don't like corporate America!" he stated emphatically. "Got no time for the bullshit that goes on there. Besides, I make a good salary."

"Seems like a waste of a good degree."

He shrugged. "I just wanted to play ball. And I did. I was the star running back for my team."

"But now you're all broken down and old. How is football helping your life now?" She laughed. "I'm sorry. I don't even know you like that."

"It's cool." He balled up his napkin and threw it at her. "You can't be much younger than me."

"I'm thirty-six."

"Okay, I'm thirty-eight with bad knees and a terrible back. So what?" He laughed.

"How did you end up in Texas?"

"Ex-wife wanted to move here. She wanted us to have a fresh start." He sighed. "I'm here now. I've built a life, own my home."

She made another mental check to her Man Menu. He owned his own home. That, too, was a plus.

"That's great," she said.

"What about you? You're a long way from home."

"I came here to attend college. I wanted to be as far away from the Bahamas as I could get! It was the only way to express my independence."

"Independence from what?"

"From my family, my parents. They would run my life if I let them. My mother would, anyway," she stated. "I promised to move home last year, when my siblings and I inherited some property. We now own a bed-and-breakfast, and they wanted me to come home and help run it. But I don't want to go back there. Like you, I've built a life here in Texas."

"I hear you."

Though Lane held a few of the traits on Whitney's Man Menu, he was coming up short on the ones that made the biggest difference. He was definitely tall, dark and handsome. He had a college degree and owned his home. But her ideal man wasn't supposed to drive a concrete truck. What would Kenya and Tasha think about that? No, the ideal man would own his own business or he'd be an executive at a Fortune 500 company. He wouldn't be a blue-collar worker with calluses on his hands. Though she didn't mind calluses so much, her friends' husbands might notice them when he shook their hands. And her ideal man certainly wouldn't be a divorcé with a kid. She had to draw the line somewhere. She'd taught eighth grade before and knew that preteens could be brutal, particularly the ones from broken homes. And even though she was enjoying his company tremendously, he definitely wasn't her type.

Chapter 6

He walked Whitney to her car and checked to see whether or not his friend had done a decent job of knocking the dent out.

He rubbed his chin. "He did good," he said.

"I thought so, too."

He took note of her round hips and the way they filled her jeans just right. A Broncos T-shirt hugged her ample breasts and small waist. He tried not to stare but found it hard to peel his eyes from her.

"What do you know about cars, anyway?"

"I know enough to know that he did a good job knocking that dent out and saved me the trouble of reporting it to my insurance company." She smiled. "Thank you."

"The least I could I do." He took a chance, grabbed her hand. Hoped she didn't pull away. She didn't. He pulled her close, wrapped his arms around her. Gave her a strong hug. He felt her hands on his back. He looked down and into her eyes, gave her a warm smile. "Thank you for meeting me here."

"Least I could do." She smiled right back at him.

He didn't ask for permission, just kissed her forehead. Her eyes were closed, and he was sure that she wanted more. But he took it slow. He let her go and reached for the driver's door of her car. She hit the lock.

"Please text me when you get home." He opened the door.

She stepped into the car, sank into the driver's seat. "I promise."

"Thank you. Drive safe." He shut her door and then stepped away. Watched as she buckled her seat belt, started the engine and pulled out of her parking space.

Instantly he regretted sharing so much. He feared that he'd run her away with talk of his ex-wife. As he made his way to his truck, he also made a conscious decision to give her some space, time, whatever. But he wouldn't pursue her. He'd been rejected once, and that was enough to last him a lifetime. He wouldn't put himself through it again—that he knew for sure.

He tossed his keys on the coffee table, pulled his shirt over his head and hit the power on the remote control. Searched the channels for ESPN. When his phone played a tune, he pulled it out of his pocket, looked at the screen.

Made it home.

Good. Thank you for letting me know, he typed.

I had a great time.

"Even after I aired all of my dirty laundry?" he whispered to himself. He couldn't help but wonder if she was just being cordial. It was a nice thing to say.

Me too, he replied.

Let's do it again.

Was she serious?

I'll call you. He typed it but knew it wasn't true. He wouldn't call her again. She was much too sweet, too beautiful, to get caught up with a guy like him. He had too many hang-ups, worries, troubles. She didn't need that in her life. She appeared to have her shit together, and the last thing he wanted to do was interfere with that.

Have a good night, was all he typed. Left it at that.

Went to the bathroom and turned on the shower.

Rest didn't come easy with a demanding job, and before he knew it, Monday morning had crept up on him. He pulled into the parking lot and backed into his usual space. Hip-hop music blasted through his speakers. He'd arrived a few minutes early, just before two in the morning—dawn nowhere in sight. So he sat there for a moment, bounced to the music. Considered sending a text to Whitney, just to say good morning, but didn't want to wake her at such an early hour.

When someone tapped on his window, it startled him. He let the window down to find Tyler standing there in an old T-shirt, a pair of jeans and work boots.

"Hey, Lane. I'm here, ready to work."

"Good," said Lane. "But don't tap on people's windows like that."

"Sorry. I didn't mean to scare you."

"Let's get you clocked in." He turned off the engine and stepped out of the car. "Follow me."

"Uncle Melvin said you always get here early. Is this the usual schedule?" asked Tyler.

"It's whatever time they need us here. Is that going to be a problem?"

"No problem at all."

"It means that on work nights, you can't hang out partying with your friends. You have to take your ass to bed so you can get up in the morning."

"I don't even have any friends here yet. So I'm good on that."

"Well, whenever you make friends. You need to be disciplined," Lane lectured the young man. "And because I'm putting myself on the line for you, don't even think about not showing up, missing work or not pulling your weight. I don't have a problem letting you go."

"I really need this job, man."

"Good! We'll see just how bad."

"I won't let you down. I promise."

"All right, then. I'll show you how to clock in, and then we'll inspect the truck."

"Cool."

Lane led the way, and Tyler followed close behind. He'd reluctantly taken the supervisory position only recently, and he was already feeling as though he'd made a mistake. He didn't like having to oversee other guys—just wanted to take care of himself. But since the previous supervisor had gone out on a disability unexpectedly, they'd asked Lane to step up in the interim.

"Just until we hire someone else," they'd pleaded.

Five months had come and gone, and his replacement still hadn't been hired. And on top of it, he despised the red-haired young man he had to report to. Blake was half Lane's age—still had milk on his breath—and cocky as hell. He micromanaged his staff of supervisors. Didn't allow them to manage their staff without interference. Lane feared that he might choke Blake if they didn't find a replacement soon.

Tyler was a quick study. His first day went exceptionally well. Lane was pleased, and relieved. He didn't need any other issues, and he didn't need dissension with his best friend because he had to let Tyler go on his first day. All was well, and he gave the young man a strong handshake.

"I'll see you tomorrow."

"Thanks for the opportunity, Lane."

"Don't thank me yet. Continue to do a good job, and we won't have any problems."

He packed his cooler into the bed of his truck. Removed his hard hat and reflective vest and threw them both into the bed, as well. Exhausted, he shrank into the driver's seat of his truck. He exhaled and let the window down, found some good riding music. Every muscle in his body ached, and all he wanted was a cold brew. He pulled his cell phone out of the pocket of his pants and checked his text messages.

Hope you're having a great day. He read the text from Whitney.

She'd sent it two hours prior, but he'd been busy training Tyler.

He replied, Busy. And yours?

I work with little people, remember? Busy as well. Headed home now.

Me too.

He wanted to invite her out for a quick bite to eat, but chances were he had another early morning. He wanted to see her beautiful face again but didn't want to rush things. Needed to take it slow. He was thinking about her too much and needed to take time and analyze those thoughts. Understand them. And moreover, attempt to dismiss them.

Chapter 7

Whitney unsnapped her bra. Pulled it through the sleeve of her shirt and tossed it onto the floor. She exhaled and rushed to the toilet. Her bladder had been about to burst as she'd sat in rush-hour traffic on the interstate. She'd almost run two red lights just to get home. She sat there for a moment contemplating dinner. Wondering if it was worth the effort to cook something or if she should just run out for fast food.

She'd just gotten back into her workout regimen because she knew she needed to maintain her current weight. It was imperative that she fit into her dress for Kenya's wedding. She'd already been fitted for the flowing red gown, with the back of it sinfully low. She wanted the silky material to hug her body effortlessly and knew that those hot wings and fries might not treat her as nicely as a baked chicken breast with a side of broccoli would.

She washed her hands and headed for the kitchen. Turned on the oven. She lit a jasmine-scented candle and found some music—Jhené Aiko. She needed something mellow to wind down from the kids, and Jhené's voice was soothing enough. After pouring herself a glass of Merlot, she seasoned a piece of chicken and tossed it into the oven.

Her phone rang, and she studied the phone number. Didn't recognize it but decided to answer anyway.

"Hello, Whitney," the male voice greeted her. "It's Jason, Kenya and Will's friend. You and I were supposed to meet at the Cheesecake Factory last week."

"Ah, Jason."

"I heard about your accident. I hope you're okay."

"I'm fine. It was just a small fender bender. Nothing serious."

"That's good to hear," said Jason. "Kenya gave me your number. I hope that's okay."

"Yeah, fine," said Whitney as she sorted through her mail.

She opened the manila-colored envelope—a formal invitation for her brother's wedding reception. The blessed event would take place at the Grove, her family's B and B on Harbour Island in the Bahamas. She had only a few weeks to find a cheap flight, a nice dress and a suitable escort. She would not be going home alone—not this time.

"I would love another opportunity to take you to dinner."

She barely heard a single word as thoughts of Lane filled her head. She wondered how he would feel about accompanying her to the islands. When another call came in, she looked at her screen. *Him.*

"I'm sorry, Jason. I have another call coming in,

and I really need to take it. Would you mind terribly if I called you back?"

"Of course not."

"Good! I'll talk to you soon." She hung up before she missed the call.

"I think I dialed the wrong number," said Lane.

"Really?"

"Yep."

"How did you manage that?"

"My phone does weird things sometimes. Like calling people randomly, just because I think about them."

"Wow, that phone is intuitive."

"Indeed." His voice smiled. "Has a mind of its own."

"How did it know that I was thinking of you at that moment?"

"That is scary," Lane laughed. "So you were thinking of me, too?"

"Sort of."

"How do you sort of think of someone?"

"It's possible."

"I don't see how. That's like being sort of pregnant or sort of married. You can't sort of think of someone. You're either thinking of them or you aren't."

"Okay, I was thinking of you!"

"Now we're getting somewhere," teased Lane. "And what exactly were you thinking?"

"Well, I got this invitation in the mail for my brother's wedding reception. He remarried his ex-wife. Long story, but the point is I need a date."

"Okay. Details."

"It's in the Bahamas in a few weeks, at my family's property there. And I would completely understand if you can't go or don't want to."

"I'd love to."

She hadn't expected that response, and so quickly. She completely figured him the type to take days and mull over things.

"Really?"

"Sure. Why not? I have plenty of vacation time. And I've never been to the Bahamas."

"Well, okay. I'll buy you a ticket, and—"

"Whoa! I can buy my own ticket."

"Okay." She didn't mean to insinuate that he couldn't. "And you'll need a passport."

"I have one, though I haven't had much of an opportunity to use it," he said. "Will I need a suit?"

"Yes. Will that be a problem?"

"No." He was a bit hesitant. "I have a suit."

He didn't strike her as the suit type, but he said he had a suit. She had no reason to doubt it. She just hoped it was an appropriate one. She didn't need any surprises. The imperious part of her wanted proof of this suit. A photograph. A description.

"Send me a pic."

"Of the suit? Are you serious?"

"Completely."

"No, sweetheart. You'll have to trust me on this one."

Trust? It was something that didn't come easy for Whitney when it pertained to men. She often ended anything that resembled a relationship before it had time to blossom. It was easier that way. And here Lane was asking her to trust him—but only with a suit, not her heart. That she could handle.

"Okay, but don't show up in anything powder blue, or with ruffles."

Lane laughed. "Should I wear white socks, or no?"

"Not a good look."

"Okay, I'll make sure I don't wear anything powder blue or ruffles or white socks."

"Whew! Now that we got that cleared up."

"Right. Now we can move on to Friday night."

"What's happening Friday night?"

"Well, I have these tickets to the Mavs game. Center court. I could take Melvin, but I'd really rather take you."

"Seriously? Are you sure you don't wanna go with your buddy? I wouldn't want to impose."

"No imposition," he said. "And besides, you're much prettier than he is."

"Okay, I'll have to agree with you there," she said. "I guess it's a date."

"I guess so."

His smile lingered in her head long after she'd hung up the phone. Lately, he was spending too much time there—in her head—and she wasn't sure what to make of it.

Chapter 8

Loud screams and stomping—those were the sounds that filled the American Airlines Center. Lane carried their beers as he cautiously followed Whitney to their seats at center court. He was always able to snag good seats. He'd done work for very influential people, like pouring concrete for a good friend of Mark Cuban's. He was even able to get good playoffs tickets as a result.

Whitney spotted their seats and slid into the row, which happened to be on the end. It was the beginning of the first quarter, and Lane checked the clock as he plopped down into his seat. He handed Whitney her beer and took note of how beautiful she looked in her college T-shirt and baseball cap turned backward on her head. Her jeans were snug and hugged those hips he was growing fond of. He couldn't help watching them as they bounced with each step when he'd followed her to their seats.

He took a long sip of his beer and adjusted his ball cap, which was also turned backward on his head. He wasn't really a Mavericks fan, but tonight he was. Especially since he wasn't particularly fond of the Memphis Grizzlies. He watched as Dirk Nowitzki stood at the free-throw line, bounced the ball a few times and sank it into the basket. Fans yelled and stomped as Dirk sprinted downcourt afterward.

"You good?" he asked Whitney. "You need anything else from the concession stand?"

"No, I'm fine. Thank you."

He was happy that she was a sports fan. It was refreshing, really, considering he lived and breathed sports. She watched the game with the intensity of a true spectator. She was cheering for the Grizzlies.

"You're a Grizzlies fan?" he asked.

"I noticed that you were going for the Mavs, so I thought I'd go for the opposite team. Give you a run for your money." She flashed that smile that he was becoming addicted to.

"So how much you got on it?" he asked.

"I got five on it."

He reached his hand out to shake hers. "Not much of a big spender."

"Okay, ten."

"How about something worth a little more, like a kiss?" He dared to throw that into the wager.

"On the cheek or the lips?"

"Lips," he said emphatically.

"With tongue?"

"Is there any other kind?"

"Okay, ten plus a kiss."

"Cool." He knew that win or lose, he was a winner. They shook on it. He was going to enjoy taking her

money and her kisses at the end of the night. He knew
the Memphis Grizzlies didn't stand a chance at winning. He grinned, sank deeper into his seat and took
another drink of his beer.

He pulled his Ford F-150 into the driveway of her
condo. He hopped out of the cab and headed around to
her door. By the time he got there, she'd already jumped
out of the truck.

"I was coming around to open the door for you. I
tried it when we got to the game, too, but you'd already
hopped out of the truck," he stated. "Not used to a man
being a gentleman?"

"I guess I just didn't expect it from…"

"From a guy like me?"

She hung her head in shame. "I'm sorry."

"It's okay. I'm always misjudged." A half smile
played in the corner of his mouth as he followed her
to the front door. "My mama taught me to be a gentleman, though."

"I see that." She searched for her key and, once she
found it, unlocked the door. Turned to him. "You wanna
come in?"

"Sure."

They stepped inside. The light scent of jasmine was
in the air. Her place was neat and cozy. Clean, with its
mahogany hardwoods and walls painted in warm colors. A white leather sectional was the focal point of the
living room. *Essence* and *Ebony* magazines were arranged neatly on the coffee table. Multicolored pillows
were everywhere. The bookshelf was filled with books
of every genre. Beautiful African art adorned her walls.
She had taste, he thought.

"Nice place. Why are you leaving?"

"I'm leasing here. And on top of it, I need a bigger space for my baby grand."

That's when he noticed the beautiful white piano in the corner of the room, taking up a great deal of her living space.

"I see. That's a serious piano."

"I'm a serious musician."

"One day you'll sing for me."

"I suppose I will."

"I look forward to it."

"I don't have beer," she stated as she dropped her purse on the counter and slipped her sneakers from her feet. "I have soda, juice, rum and vodka."

"Well, you just said the magic word. *Vodka*. That's my drink." He took a seat on the sofa. "You have cranberry juice, by chance?"

"You're in luck. I do." She smiled. "Make yourself at home, and I'll fix us a drink."

He sat on the edge of the sofa closest to the television and resisted the urge to reach for the remote control and search for ESPN. Instead he stood and walked over to her stereo and turned it on. It was a vintage piece, the kind that played old-school albums as well as CDs.

"This is nice," he said.

"I found it at my little antiques store in Plano," she said. "A rare piece. I like to collect rare pieces."

"Nice."

"Find us some music," she said as she carried drinks into the living room, placed them on coasters on the coffee table.

She sat on the sofa, her legs curled underneath her as she watched him. He sorted through her collection of albums, and when he found one, he looked at her and smiled. She tried to pretend that she hadn't been staring, but he knew she had. She was sizing him up, he thought—trying to see if he fit the bill. He caught her eye and then slipped the album from its cover and placed it on the record player.

"What do you know about this?" he asked as Donny Hathaway's voice resonated through the room.

"What do you know about it?" she asked and took a sip of her wine.

"I know that my mother used to wear him out when I was younger," he said. "Every Friday night, a game of cards and old music. Mostly the blues, but some artists like Donny Hathaway, Marvin Gaye and a few others."

"My parents entertained a lot. But I grew up listening to old Bahamian artists. George Symonette, especially."

"Never heard of him."

"It's okay. I listened to enough of him for the both of us." She laughed. "It was only in college that I discovered some of the old-school American artists like Donny, Marvin and others. My girlfriend Kenya has an old soul and used to play their music."

"I see." He relaxed on the sofa again, took a sip of his drink. "She has good taste."

"She does," said Whitney. "It took me a while to locate some of those old albums, but my brother Nate lives in Atlanta and found a record store that sells them."

"How many siblings do you have?" he asked, and regretted it. He knew that asking about her siblings would only lead to her asking about his.

"It's six of us. I have three brothers and two sisters. Most of us live in the States, except for my younger sister, Jasmine, who runs our B and B on Harbour Island. And my sister Alyson, who now lives in the islands, too," she said. "Once upon a time, I was supposed to go back to there and help run our family business, but that didn't happen."

"You don't want to return to the islands." He remembered her mentioning it before. "Why not?"

"Not for good. I kind of like Texas. I've gotten settled here," she said.

"Me, too," said Lane.

"How many siblings do you have?" she inquired.

His heart began to beat at a fast pace. It was a subject that he hated to talk about. Siblings. And especially his brother. He knew that he'd have to tell her about Tye one day, but tonight wouldn't be it.

"There were three of us. I had two older brothers, Clint and Tye. Clint lives in Saint Louis. My brother Tye is deceased."

"I'm sorry."

"Don't be. It's okay."

He knew he had to change the subject, and quick. Talk of Tye always changed his mood and he didn't want that tonight. They'd had a great night. Besides the fact that the Mavericks had lost and he'd lost the bet, he was having a nice night. He figured he'd won anyway, because before the night was over, he'd be getting kissed real good. That is, if she didn't renege on their wager.

She must've sensed his discomfort. "You owe me ten bucks!" she exclaimed.

He stood, dug into the pocket of his jeans. Pulled out a wad of cash, removed the money clip. He peeled a ten-dollar bill from the stack and handed it to her. "Happy?" he asked.

"No," she said. "You owe me a kiss, as well."

He held his hand out to her. She reached for it and he pulled her up from the sofa. He wrapped his arms around her waist and pulled her into him. The fragrance she wore was intoxicating. His nose touched hers and electricity rushed through his body. His lips found hers. He kissed her and then parted her lips with his tongue and allowed it to dance inside her mouth—just as he'd promised.

Chapter 9

She lay in bed, staring at the ceiling. Usually on Saturday morning, she would be up, preparing a protein shake before heading to the gym. She usually had a laundry list of errands that needed to be run. But this morning, she relaxed. Thoughts of Lane danced in her head. She thought of how those strong arms had wrapped themselves tightly around her. It felt good there—safe. She thought of his dark face and silky, smooth skin. His smile had brightened the room more than it already had been. And his kiss was sweeter than she could remember a kiss being before. Her hormones had stirred when his tongue danced in her mouth. That never happened.

Whatever this was she was feeling, she needed to dismiss it. She'd invited him to the islands, but only because she needed a date. After that, they'd go their separate ways and she'd go back to life as she knew it.

He wasn't her type. She knew it. He had barely any of the traits on her Man Menu. Sure, he had potential, but she was so tired of running into guys who had *potential*. She needed a complete package. She had no desire of bringing anyone up to speed or waiting around for someone to live up to her standards. Yes, she had standards. And if she didn't stand by them, then what was the point of having them?

She got up, washed and moisturized her face. Pulled her hair into a ponytail and headed to the kitchen to brew a pot of Ethiopian coffee—the kind that she special-ordered from a local roaster. She loved how the aroma filled her home. She would pass on the gym workout—didn't feel much like lifts, squats or crunches. And her errands could wait. Instead she needed a new swimsuit for the beach. And she wondered if Patrice, her hairstylist, could fit her in for a last-minute appointment. She looked at her nails and thought she could use a manicure, and her toes needed a pedicure, like, months ago. A couple of new outfits wouldn't hurt either.

She expected Patrice's shop to be packed on a Saturday morning. And it was. There was barely anywhere to sit in the waiting area. But she was grateful that she was able to fit her in, though she would pay for it with the long wait. Luckily, Kenya and Tasha were both there for their standing Saturday-morning appointments. At least she'd have someone to talk to while waiting. She snagged a seat in between them.

"Well, look who's here," said Tasha. "I haven't seen you in forever."

"I know." She gave her friend a tight squeeze. "How have you been, honey?"

"Not bad. Work is a beast!"

"I'm still coming by to see you about my portfolio. I'd like to do some rearranging of my investments," said Whitney.

"Please do, sweetie. We really need to get your portfolio in order. You won't be young enough to run around chasing five-year-olds forever, you know?"

"Plan for the future. I know."

"What are you doing here?" Kenya asked. "This is your gym time."

"I know, but I needed my hair done," said Whitney as she held out her hands in front of her friend, "and these nails."

"You couldn't care less about your nails. I usually have to drag you to the nail shop kicking and screaming."

"Well, the time has come that I can't neglect them any longer."

"They are pretty bad, Whit." Tasha grabbed her hand to give her nails a closer look.

"You're up to something!" said Kenya, with a raised eyebrow.

"Is there a man involved?" asked Tasha.

"You talked to Jason, didn't you?" Kenya asked.

"Who's Jason?" Tasha was on the edge of her seat by then.

"He's Will's friend." Kenya grinned. "A real cutie! Owns his own business. Has just about every damn thing on our Man Menu."

"Really?" Tasha smiled wickedly. "Do tell."

"There's nothing to tell." Whitney decided not to tell them that they had it completely wrong.

It wasn't Jason who had her switching up her entire routine, fussing over hair and nails, her hormones completely out of whack. No, she'd barely even talked to Jason. But she was enjoying the fact that they didn't have a clue.

"Is he going with you to the Bahamas? To your brother's reception?" Kenya asked.

"You're taking a man to the Bahamas?" asked Tasha. "Do you even know him like that?"

"Oh my God, how romantic! I wish I could get Will to take me to one of those exotic islands. I need a vacation so desperately."

"Yes, you do!" Whitney finally got a word in edgewise. "You're going to Bermuda for your honeymoon."

"I know, but that's so far away."

"Your wedding will be here before you know it." Whitney gave her friend a warm smile and grabbed her hand.

She was genuinely happy for Kenya, though she knew that the couple would have challenges in their impending marriage. Will was married to his career. Barely had time to take Kenya to a movie, or even out for a bite to eat. She'd spent many a night with Kenya—the two of them sipping on a bottle of Riesling as Kenya poured her heart out about how neglected she felt. She was under the impression that marriage would somehow repair their problems or fill the gap between them. Whitney knew that it wouldn't, but she didn't have the courage to break her friend's heart.

Will was always going to be a workaholic. Just as Tasha's husband, Louis, was always going to be a womanizer. And the thought of both men shook Whitney to her core. Watching her friends endure such pain in their relationships was what made her steer clear of anything that looked like a commitment. She guarded her heart like the Secret Service guarded the president of the United States—with her life. With her friends she pretended to look for that perfect man who had every single quality on her Man Menu—but secretly she hoped that she never found him. And if any guy ever came close, she looked for something—the smallest *something*— that would disqualify him.

"When do you leave?" asked Kenya.

"In a couple of weeks."

"Take lots of pictures."

"Be careful. You barely know this guy," said Tasha. "I watch the Investigation Discovery channel, girl, and I don't wanna see you on it."

"Tasha, I'm ready for you, honey," said Patrice.

Whitney was glad when Patrice finally called Tasha. She loved her friend, but she could take only so much of her.

"I'm not going to the Bahamas with Jason," Whitney whispered to Kenya.

"What?" Kenya eyeballed her. "Who, then?"

Whitney simply smiled.

"The truck driver?" Kenya asked.

"Shhh!" Whitney said. "You don't have to say it like that."

"Well, how should I say it? You're the one with this Man Menu that no one can seem to live up to."

"We all live by the Man Menu."

"You certainly do. No man can ever live up to yours."

"I know. But I have to admit, I kind of like him."

"Really?"

"He's fun and genuine. There's something there, like we have this chemistry. I can't explain it, Kenya. It's like I've known him forever."

"Wow." Kenya placed her palm on Whitney's fore-head. "You don't have a fever."

"Stop. I'm serious," said Whitney. "When I kissed him last night…"

"You've kissed him already?"

Kenya grabbed a magazine from the coffee table, covered her face with it. "Well, actually, he kissed me, but I wanted more. So much more. There, I said it."

Kenya snatched the magazine from her. Smiled. "Well, damn."

"I know."

"That's why you're all up in the beauty shop, trying to get cute. Fussing over your trifling fingernails."

"Don't tell Tasha," whispered Whitney.

"You don't have to worry about me saying a word. I don't want to hear her mouth."

"Me neither," said Whitney. "Besides, we're just having fun."

"Of course."

"I needed a date for my brother's reception, and he just happened to be available. That's all it is."

"Right."

"No, really. You know I could never be serious about anyone. I run them all away. You know that." She said it in a lighthearted manner but knew it was the truth.

"You'll give in to the right one. And you'll know he's the right one, too," said Kenya. "Just like I knew that my Will was the right one. He's a good man, and I can't wait to marry him."

When Kenya was called to the shampoo bowl for a wash, Whitney exhaled. She'd been so busy trying to convince her friend that this thing with Lane was nothing, when really she was trying to convince herself.

When she left Patrice's shop, she was happy with her hairstyle. It was somewhat of an edgy style—something that she would normally never have had the courage to try, but she'd decided to step outside her conservative box a bit. She'd heard rave reviews from a few of the teachers at her school about a new nail shop in the Arts District. She didn't usually frequent that part of town but decided to give it a try. She pulled into the parking lot but sat in her car for a moment—enjoyed the last few minutes of Tamia's "You Put a Move on My Heart." It made her think of Lane. He was certainly putting a move on her heart.

When she looked up, she spotted Will, Kenya's fiancé, walking out of the ice-cream shop. She held her head low, didn't want him to see her. She had no intention of explaining why she'd blown his friend off. He seemed like a nice enough guy, but she'd known immediately that he wasn't her type. Or maybe he could've been her type, but she wasn't at all interested in finding out. Her interests lay elsewhere.

She averted her eyes to the dashboard in her car, pretended to change the station on her radio. When she looked up, Will was standing right in front of her car, and a tall bronze-colored model-like woman had her arm looped inside his. He wrapped his arm around the woman's neck and pulled her face to his—kissed her passionately. She touched his face with her palm and then wiped the traces of lipstick from his lips. They laughed about something and then the woman walked away toward her two-door Mercedes-Benz and hopped into it. Will watched her every move like a lovesick puppy and then headed toward his SUV.

Whitney was frozen. She should've said something, confronted him, cursed him, even. But she couldn't move. She was stuck, and she tried to make sense of what she'd just witnessed. Her heart beat fast and her hand trembled as she reached for her cell phone and began to search for Kenya's phone number. She rested her head against the leather seat and wondered how she was ever going to tell her dearest friend that the man she intended to marry in just a few months was a cheat.

Her mind went back to the time in college when she'd fallen out with Kenya over a man. Foster Payne was the handsome quarterback who'd dated Kenya but was secretly making passes at her. She'd immediately told Kenya about it but was accused of trying to steal her man.

"He told me you were making passes at him," Kenya had accused.

"And you believe him instead of me?"

"Yes." Kenya had stated it emphatically.

"Fine. Be stupid, then," Whitney spat and vowed never to speak to her again.

As it turned out, Whitney hadn't been the only one of Kenya's friends that Foster had made passes at. His sole purpose in attending college was to party and sow his wild oats. Kenya eventually got over Foster, but the aftermath had left their friendship a bit unsettled—for at least half of their sophomore year, they barely spoke. But once they hashed out their differences, they'd promised that a man would never come between them again. Yet here she was again, faced with having to repeat history and hand Kenya some bad news about her guy. Only this time, the stakes were higher. They weren't young college kids anymore, and this wasn't about a boy sowing his wild oats. This was about a man who was a few months from meeting her at the altar.

She tossed her phone against the leather seat. Couldn't bring herself to make the call. No. If she was going to risk their friendship again, it was something that needed to be done in person.

Chapter 10

He sat in the chair, a cape draped around him. The buzz from the clippers filled his ear as Cleveland lined up his fade.

"I think the Chiefs can still pull it off," he said.

"Just like you said that Sanaa Lathan was better-looking than Halle Berry." Melvin folded the *Dallas Morning* newspaper and pointed it at Lane. "You need your head checked."

"She is," said Lane. "And a much nicer body, too."

"Psst." Melvin blew wind through his lips. "Man, you are crazy."

"I have to agree," Cleveland chimed in. "Much better body."

"I think Halle's kind of played out," Tim said as he trimmed Old Man Jackson's mustache with a straight razor.

"I don't know about that, young man. Halle Berry is a good-looking woman," said Old Man Jackson.

"Can we get back to the NFL? I got some money on who's going to the Super Bowl, and it ain't the Chiefs," said Tim.

"You are crazy!" Lane exclaimed. "Man, the Chiefs are seven and three."

"Raiders going all the way this year," said Big Steve, who was patiently waiting for his turn in the chair.

"I don't know. Chiefs might have a chance," said Cleveland. "But my money's on the Broncos."

"You have a right to your opinion," said Lane with a chuckle.

"Be still if you want this line straight," said Cleveland.

"You mess up my line, and that's your ass!" said Lane, and laughter filled the room. "I need it to be perfect."

"Yep, for Bahamas," said Melvin as he opened the newspaper again and held it up to his face.

"What's that? Bahamas?" Cleveland asked.

"More like *who's that?*" said Melvin. "Bahamas is a person."

"Who's Bahamas?"

"Just this little woman I met. She ran into my truck…"

"She didn't see that big-ass truck you drive?" Cleveland asked, and the room filled with laughter again.

"She was a little distracted," said Lane. "Look at all this goodness. You would be distracted, too."

"Aw, man." Melvin threw his hand toward Lane.

"She got him love struck?" Cleveland asked Melvin with a laugh.

"Hell no, I'm not love struck!"

"Took her to the Mavs game last night…knowing good and damn well that was my seat!"

"Man, jealousy doesn't look good on you," said Lane.

"Not jealous, but you know chicks don't appreciate basketball."

"Well, this one does," said Lane. "She knows a little something about sports."

"Whoa!" said Melvin. "Defensive, aren't we?"

"You like this girl, huh?" asked Cleveland as he loosened the cape from around Lane's neck and brushed away the stray hairs.

"She's all right. We hung out a little bit. Nothing more than that."

"Mmm-hmm," Melvin sang. "He's catching feelings."

"No! Never that," said Lane.

"He's going with her to the Bahamas, to meet her family."

"What?" everyone in the barbershop asked in harmony as all eyes landed on Lane.

"It's not what you think. I'm her date for this little gathering...her brother's wedding reception or something."

"That's a long way to travel for a date," said Tim.

"I have some vacation time to burn. Really, it's no big deal."

"Get off the man's case," said Old Man Jackson. "You need to live, son. Go have a good time. Don't let these fellas get to you. If you like the woman, then you just do. Nothing wrong with that."

"Exactly," said Lane as he stood, brushed his clothes. He reached for Old Man Jackson's hand. "Thank you, Mr. Jackson."

"Anytime, young man."

"Let's go, Big Head," said Lane to Melvin after he paid for his haircut.

* * *

Lane and Melvin took their usual seats at the bar. Max's was always packed on a weekend. It was where crowds gathered to watch sports and to drink for hours.

"Gimme a Heineken, Max," said Lane. "And give this chump one of those little sissy drinks."

Max laughed as he set a beverage napkin in front of each of them.

"I'll take a Bud Light, Max. And a shot of tequila," said Melvin.

"What are you doing behind the bar, anyhow?" Lane asked.

"One of my guys didn't make it in today," said Max as he placed a beer in front of Lane and another one in front of Melvin. "Good help is hard to find."

"You're a jack-of-all-trades." Lane turned up his beer.

"You have to be in this business. Sometimes I have to roll up my sleeves and wash a few dishes, too," said Max.

"I hear you," said Lane. "It's why I love this place. Owner is down to earth."

"It feels like home," Melvin added.

"Well, I appreciate your business. Both of you have been coming here for as long as I can remember."

"Always will."

Max leaned in, and spoke almost in a whisper. "That is, if we remain open. It's getter harder by the day to keep these doors open."

"It looks like business is booming. Always crowded when I come in here."

"When that new investor came in and bought up the shopping plaza, he raised my rent. Made it almost impossible for me to make ends meet. Wants to drive some of the older businesses out of here. Turn this place into something fancy that caters to the higher class."

"What? Max's has been here for years," said Lane.

"A cornerstone of the neighborhood," Melvin tossed back his shot of tequila.

"These young, ambitious developers don't care about that. They're about making money. That's it," said Max. "He's waiting for me to lose the space so that he can turn it into something else. He's already alluded to that."

"You do so much for this community, though, Max. Like feeding the hungry and those clothes drives."

"And what about that barbeue you held out back last summer to raise money for that children's shelter?"

"Yeah, I have to take care of my community," said Max. "What about you, Lane? You do a lot for this community, too, man. You're always volunteering at the shelters. And you do that Big Brother thing with the kids year round. That's admirable."

"I have a kid of my own, and I don't wanna see any child go without."

"That's right, man," said Max. "Wherever I fall short, I know you'll take care of the rest."

"Damn right," said Lane. He and Max's fists touched in agreement.

"Maybe you can take Max's off my hands. I'll sell it to you at a good price."

"What are you talking about...sell Max's." Lane laughed, but Max wasn't laughing.

"My wife and I are divorcing, and..."

"What?" Lane and Melvin said it in unison.

"Yeah, we've kept it under wraps for a while, but it's happening. And with everything that's going on, I can't afford to keep this place going. I'm sinking every day."

"But you and the missus...you've been married forever." Lane was disappointed. Seeing the two of them in Max's together over the years had given him somewhat of a glimmer of hope that love really existed.

"Some good things come to an end."

He felt some type of way about Max's news. Couldn't shake it. "You're serious."

"Hey, man, you told me once that you had some money put away—and you were looking for something to invest in. Well, here you go!" said Max. "I'd rather see you keep Max's alive than the developer transforming it into something else."

"You did say that," Melvin agreed as he took a sip of his beer.

"It would be a smooth transition. And I would give you a good price," said Max as he grabbed Lane by the shoulder. "Give it some thought."

Max wiped down the bar and then disappeared into the kitchen. Lane entertained the thought of his proposition for a moment, but then his thoughts immediately drifted back to the talk of divorce. People were always splitting up, he thought. Nobody stayed together. His father had split when he was five. And then his own divorce left him emotionally drained. What was appealing about love and commitment, if people never actually committed? It was a worthless waste of time for all parties involved. However, the thought of owning a business was appealing, but did he really want to own a bar? And could he afford the rent and the staff? And would he be driven insane like Max had been with all the craziness that had gone on over the years?

He would give it some thought, but for now he needed to focus on this impending trip to the Bahamas. A trip that he was feeling less and less excited about now.

Chapter 11

Her heart ached. Every inch of it. She knew that she needed to talk to Kenya before leaving for the Bahamas, but knowing and doing were two very different things. And so far, she'd held on to this secret for two weeks and carefully avoided Kenya's calls. Her text messages were short and to the point—not their usual friendly banter. She thought about that day and how she'd started out driving toward Kenya's condo in North Dallas but turned her car around in midstream. Headed home instead. She knew it was wrong, but avoiding the inevitable seemed easier. She didn't want to lose her friend again.

She tossed her swimsuit into the bag and sipped on a glass of Riesling as Lalah Hathaway's voice soothed her soul. She shook her head. Just when she thought there was a glimmer of hope for love, she'd lost it in an instant. She couldn't remember ever truly loving anyone after Gregory, and if it were left up to her, she'd never love again. Love was too painful.

She'd picked up her phone a dozen times over the past week—wanted to call Lane and tell him that she didn't need him to accompany her to the Bahamas after all. She was fully capable of making the trip alone. She hated that she'd even invited him in the first place. Hated that she'd bumped into his cement truck to begin with. But now that she had invited him, she would go along with their original plans. She'd take an Uber and meet Lane at DFW Airport at the crack of dawn. Get this over with so that she could get back to her single solitude—her life before handsome truck drivers existed in it. Back to her life where the only men who existed were the ones who could never live up to her Man Menu.

He was an early bird. Had already texted that he was waiting for her at the security checkpoint. He gave her the widest grin when he saw her—a genuine one that he'd given her the last time she saw him. It made her heart sink. It was sweet, and one that said *It's so good to see you.* Though he wasn't a man who laid on the compliments like plaster, she could tell that he was pleased with what he saw.

"You made it," he said and pulled her into an embrace and kissed her cheek. His cologne delighted her nose.

"Of course," she said. "Were you hoping I didn't show up?"

"No," he said. "Were you considering not showing up?"

"No."

"Well, good." He grabbed her carry-on bag and draped it over his shoulder.

Always a gentleman, she noted. Couldn't knock him

in that area, for sure. He touched the small of her back as he pushed her to go ahead of him toward the TSA agent.

She sat in the window seat and lifted the blind. "I know men have an issue with sitting in the middle seat, so I'd be happy to switch seats with you if necessary."

"I'm good," he said confidently.

"Okay, because I really like the view as we descend in the Bahamas. But I've seen it a bunch of times, so again, I'll let you have the window."

"I'm good," he said again with a laugh. "I can see the view from here. Relax."

"Okay." She placed her phone in airplane mode and stuck it into her purse.

She'd wanted desperately to be awake when they descended, but by the time her eyes opened, the plane was taxiing the runway and headed toward the gate at Governor's Harbour Airport.

She smacked the back of her hand against Lane's chest, as if they were old friends. "Why didn't you wake me before we landed?"

"Sorry." He smiled. "You were sleeping so good I didn't want to interrupt you."

"I was tired," she admitted. Her sleep habits weren't the greatest. She had early mornings and late nights. Mostly up thinking about things she couldn't do anything about, like the lives of the children in her class. Some of them seemed to have trouble at home. She knew it in her heart but wasn't able to prove any of it—and it drove her crazy.

"I know. You were snoring...and drooling."

"I was not snoring or drooling!" She touched her mouth to check for drool.

"Okay, maybe not drooling, but definitely snoring."

She shook her head and then peered out of the window. She had anxiety just thinking that in just a few minutes she'd be hugging her father. She hadn't seen him in almost a year—not since her parents' anniversary party last spring. It was when she and all of her siblings had come home to the islands, and she'd been surprised to see that her brother Edward was reuniting with his ex-wife. They'd found love a second time around and here she was back on the islands for their wedding reception.

Her father stood tall in his khaki pants, a button-down sky-blue shirt and a pair of loafers. His salt-and-pepper hair looked more salt than pepper, and he looked thinner than he had the last time she saw him. His wide grin was the thing that she missed most about him, and he gave her one when he spotted her. He opened his arms wide and she ran into them—never too old to run into her daddy's arms. She hugged him tight, just like she did the first time he walked her to elementary school.

"Hey, Daddy!" she said, her face buried against his chest.

"Hello, baby," he said in his baritone Bahamian dialect.

She held on to his waist and turned to find Lane standing close by.

"Daddy, this is my friend Lane," she said.

"Hello, son." He reached for Lane's hand and gave it a strong squeeze. "Paul John Talbot."

"Pleased to meet you, sir," said Lane. "Lane Martin."

"Good to meet you, as well," said Paul John, and gave his daughter a rise of the eyebrow.

Paul John rarely said much about what his children did in their lives, but he always took notice of everything. Whitney never brought anyone home to the islands, so she was sure her father was curious about Lane and how he'd gained the honor of accompanying her home. But he didn't waste time with questions. He grabbed her suitcase and headed outside toward his pickup truck. Her father, a former physician, had driven that truck for too many years. Clearly he could afford something newer but loved that truck. Whitney and Lane followed Paul John and he tossed her bags in the bed and motioned for Lane to do the same.

Paul John drove down Queen's Highway, his old-school Bahamian music playing loudly on the stereo. Whitney, who sat in between the two men, changed the station to a more contemporary one. Her father shook his head and smiled. He knew his middle daughter quite well. He knew all three of his daughters well— probably better than they knew themselves. Jasmine was the youngest—outgoing and adventurous, always uncertain of how amazing she was. Alyson, the oldest and the diva of the family. Alyson had no filter. Her rough edges carefully hid her insecurities. Whitney was unlike either of her sisters, in that she was quite sure of herself and didn't have very many insecurities.

Being the middle child had taught her strength, to stand on her own—it was she who didn't require as much attention. Yet her father always gave her a nod, a wink or some gesture to let her know that he recognized her existence. He had a way of making every person in the family feel just as important as the next. That's what she loved about him. That, and the fact that she could talk to him about any and everything and he never judged. She rested her head on his shoulder.

"Glad you're home," he said.

"Me, too."

"You two are staying at the house, right?" he asked.

"At the Grove," she corrected him, referring to her family's bed-and-breakfast.

"Oh," he said.

She raised her head. "What?"

"Your mum was expecting you to stay at the house. Got your rooms all fixed up nice, ya know?"

"Really?" said Whitney, "I'm pretty sure I told her we were staying at the Grove."

"You might have, darling, but I tell you, she's expecting you to stay at the house."

Whitney sighed. She'd always stayed at the house when she'd come home in the past—*alone*. But this time, she wanted private time with Lane and she knew that wouldn't be possible at her childhood home. Her mother would be all in her business, and watching her like a hawk. The two wouldn't have one single private conversation—not with Beverly Talbot around. She was her mother's favorite. She knew it, and so did her other siblings. Her mother had been a teacher in her former life, and often Whitney felt as if her mother lived vicariously through her. But sometimes that felt like more of a curse than a blessing.

"Dear God," Whitney mumbled under her breath.

The moment she walked into the house, she recognized the smell of her mother's johnnycakes. She heard the sounds of contemporary Caribbean music. Beverly Talbot met them in the living room, wiping her hands on an apron wrapped around her waist.

"Hello, baby," she exclaimed.

"Mother!" Whitney gave her mother a tight squeeze.

"You lookin' good."

"Thank you, Mum."

"And who do we have here?" Beverly gave Lane a wide grin.

"This is Lane. Lane, this is my mother, Beverly Talbot."

"Nice meeting you, ma'am," said Lane as he took Beverly's hand in his. "You're way more beautiful than I expected."

"He's quite the charmer," said Beverly to Whitney with a smile. "Come on. I know you're both hungry."

"Starved!" said Whitney.

"The others will be here shortly. But you can grab a small bite before supper."

"Yes!" Whitney exclaimed.

Paul John gave Lane a pat on the back. "Follow me, son. I'll show you where to put the bags."

Whitney followed her mother to the kitchen. Lane followed Paul John.

"He's cute," said Beverly. "I don't think I ever remember you bringing a young man home."

"He's just a friend, Mum."

"Is he a teacher, too?"

"No. He drives a truck."

"I see," said Beverly. "And he makes a good living from that?"

"A very good one," said Whitney as she began to search through the cupboards. "Is there any rum in the house?"

"Of course. I made your rum punch." Beverly pointed at the refrigerator.

"Good." She grabbed a glass and poured herself a drink.

She was grateful for rum punch. It was what she missed most about the Bahamas. That and the beach. But mostly the rum. And she was going to need plenty of it to get through the weekend.

Chapter 12

The Bahamas was way more beautiful than Lane could've imagined, with its clear blue skies and the scent of the ocean floating through the air. He couldn't understand why Whitney had chosen to leave this place—her home. It was far more beautiful than Saint Louis, or Texas for that matter. His first trip out of the country, and he wondered why he'd waited so long.

"I love it here," he told Paul John as they reclined on the front porch, a Bahamian beer in his hand.

"I love it, too," said Paul John. "Would never live anywhere else."

"Beautiful home you have, too, sir."

"Thank you. It's where we raised all six of our children. It's old and in need of a few repairs, but it's home," said Paul John. "Where do you call home?"

"Saint Louis."

"Old Saint Louie. I've been through there as a young

man. I played in a band in my younger days, and we played Saint Louis a few times."

"It's a great place to call home. My mother is still there," said Lane.

"And your father?"

"He's still there, too. But I don't acknowledge him much. He wasn't around when I needed him most."

"I see." Paul John leaned back in his chair, gave his beard a tug and thought about Lane's words. "Is he around now?"

"He's in a nursing home, too sick to care for himself. I don't think I will ever forgive him for the way he treated my mother, or for abandoning us."

Paul John shook his head up and down. "Forgiveness is a funny thing, ya know. Everyone thinks that it's for the wrongdoer. Thinks it lets them off the hook. Truth is, forgiveness is really for the forgiver—to give them peace, to make them whole."

"I'm at peace."

"I don't doubt that you are, son. But I learned a long time ago that it's best to let some things go. And forgiveness does us all a world of good." Paul John stood, headed for the door. "You want another beer, son?"

"Yes, sir."

Lane sat there and reflected on what Paul John said. He was right. There were some things that just needed to be let go. And he would…someday. He enjoyed chatting with Whitney's father. However, he wasn't looking forward to meeting her siblings. When he agreed to accompany her on the trip, he'd thought of it as a chance to spend some time with her, get to know her better, not meet the entire family. It wasn't as if they were in a relationship. He was looking for fun. But since he was here, he'd make the best of it.

* * *

Dinner was a medley of baked fish, peas and rice, Bahamian macaroni and cheese, and something that Lane had never tasted in his life—conch fritters. He sat at the table across from Whitney and sipped on a glass of port wine while Caribbean music played on the old stereo. The table was filled with loud chatter from Whitney's siblings and in-laws who had made it home for their brother's reception. To his right, Whitney's brother Nate grilled her about why she rarely made it home.

"I'm home just as much as you are!" she exclaimed.

"Where were you when Mother turned sixty-five? We had a huge dinner. It was like an...event, for chrissake! And what about Independence Day?"

"I can't come home for every event or holiday. I have a job."

"We all have jobs," said Nate.

"I have a real one, a nine-to-five."

"Are you saying my job isn't real?"

"No, I'm not saying that at all," said Whitney.

"Leave her alone," said Whitney's younger brother, seated to the left of Lane. He stuffed macaroni and cheese into his mouth. "She was here for Mother and Pop's anniversary party last spring."

"Thank you, Denny!" Whitney blew him a kiss.

"She was actually supposed to come help out at the Grove once we got it up and running," Whitney's youngest sister, Jasmine, chimed in. "She reneged."

"I didn't renege," said Whitney. "I ended up teaching summer school last year."

"And singing at some club," said Whitney's oldest sister, Alyson. "And I heard that she was thinking of singing as a career."

"What's this about singing as a career?" asked Beverly Talbot. "She would never leave teaching to go chasing some pipe dream. Right, Whit?"

"It's just something that I like to do on the side," said Whitney. "Now, can we attack someone else?"

"No one's attacking you," said Jasmine.

"Tell me more about this singing," said Nate, "because I remember being damn near beat up… Excuse me, Mother…Pop. I was nearly stoned for wanting to pursue a career in art!"

"I admit, I wasn't too keen on the art thing," said Beverly. "We sent you to college to study engineering."

"And look at me now, Mother. Doing something I love, and it's actually paying the bills."

Beverly gave her son a light smile.

"Has anyone heard from Edward and when he and Savannah are supposed to arrive?" asked Alyson. "Why are we all here, and they aren't? Isn't this *their* blessed weekend?"

"They're scheduled to arrive later this evening," said Beverly.

"Maybe I should've waited and come over later this evening with Samson."

"No, Samson probably wanted you to leave. I'm sure he needed a break from you!" Nate laughed.

"No, I needed a break from him!" Alyson exclaimed. "He was getting on my nerves."

"I find that hard to believe."

"Go to hell, Nathan Talbot."

"I'm just saying." Nate laughed. "You're not the easiest person to get along with."

"I just have high standards, and most people aren't able to meet them."

Lane smiled at the banter between Whitney and

her family. It made him miss his own family. He felt guilty about not returning home in so long. His mother had been pressuring him about coming home, and he'd found every excuse not to. Too many memories, too much heartache.

"And what's your story—Lane, is it?" Alyson asked before taking a long drink of her wine.

"My story?" Lane asked.

"Yes, what do you do? Who's your family? Where are you from?"

"I drive a cement truck. And my family? The Martins from Saint Louis, Missouri."

Jasmine smiled at Lane. "You pour cement? I bet my hubby would love to have a chat with you. He's in construction and always looking for someone to recruit for his many projects."

"Your mother and father still back in Saint Louis, honey?" asked Beverly.

"Yes, ma'am," Lane said. "My mother retired from the old Chrysler plant there. They've since closed down, but she worked there for many years."

"What is she doing now?"

"Church stuff. Volunteer work."

"Have you met his mother, Whitney?" Beverly continued to pry.

"No, Mother, I haven't," said Whitney and then turned to her sister. "Jazzy, can you pass me the peas and rice, please?"

Jasmine passed the bowl across the table.

"Why not?" asked Beverly.

"Beverly, I think we're all ready for dessert now," said Paul John. He seemed to sense his daughter's discomfort. "Would you like for me to help?"

Beverly rolled her eyes at her husband, who was

obviously trying to distract her from her line of questioning.

She stood. "No, Paul, I can manage."

"You're sure?"

"Completely," she said and then headed for the kitchen.

Lane exhaled. And he could've sworn he saw Whitney exhale, too.

Chapter 13

After dinner, the women put food away and cleaned the kitchen, while the men retreated to the front porch. Soon the women gathered in the living room and chatted about nothing, and Whitney thought it was time she rescued Lane from her family. Thought they'd take a walk along the beach or take the ferry over to Harbour Island. She went to the front door and peeked out. He was seated in between her father and brothers, a beer in his hand. His laughter told her that he was having a good time—fit right in. Her oldest brother, Edward, who'd finally arrived, wrapped his arm around Lane's shoulder and they looked like old friends.

She didn't want to interrupt, so she backed away from the door, went into the kitchen and poured herself another rum punch. Joined the other women in the living room.

"Thought you were going for a walk on the beach with Lane," said Beverly.

"Looks like he's having such a good time, I didn't want to interrupt."

"I like him," said Jasmine with a warm smile.

"Me, too," said Savannah, Whitney's sister-in-law, who had finally arrived from Florida. She held on to the bowl of her wineglass. Gave Whitney a wink. "Edward seems to like him, too."

"Well, don't get too cozy with him. She's made it very clear that they're *just friends*," said Alyson.

"We are."

"I find it hard to understand why you would bring a man home to meet your family if you have no intentions of something long-term," said Alyson.

"I wanted a date for Edward and Savannah's reception."

"It's okay to bring a friend home," said Jasmine. "What's wrong with that?"

"She's never brought anyone home…not even what's-his-name." Alyson waved her hand.

"Gregory!" Jasmine exclaimed and then frowned. "He was a jerk."

"He broke her heart. It's why she's gun-shy. Won't give anyone else her heart," said Alyson, who seemed to be an expert on the matter. "I don't blame you, girl. Men are overrated."

"How can you say that when you have a wonderful husband?" Whitney asked her.

"He's okay. Gets under my skin most days, though."

Whitney laughed inside. She knew that her sister could be impossible and the truth was probably that she got under his skin.

"Alyson!" Beverly exclaimed.

"It's the truth, Mother," she said and then poured herself another glass of wine.

"Well, I love my husband!" said Jasmine. "He's an amazing man."

"I love my husband, too," said Savannah. "I've always loved Edward, even after we divorced. I'm so thankful for our second chance."

"I'm happy for you both," said Whitney. "I've always loved you, Savannah. Just like a sister."

"I've always loved you, too!" Savannah wrapped her arms around Whitney. "I've always loved you all."

Jasmine blew Savannah a kiss.

"Edward was so pathetic without you," said Alyson. "He was like a lovesick puppy when he thought he'd lost you. Showed up on my doorstep trying to enlist my help. I'm glad you finally rescued him from his misery."

"If that's your way of saying you've always loved me, Alyson, I'll take it." Savannah smiled at her sister-in-law.

Alyson sighed. Shook her head. "Yes, I've always loved you, too."

The women all laughed heartily. Alyson played hard, but they all knew that beneath her hard exterior was a loving woman.

When Whitney could no longer keep her eyes open, she retreated to the old bedroom that she'd shared with Jasmine. She wasn't surprised to find that it was pretty close to the way they'd left it when they both went away to college. It was untouched unless she or Jasmine came home for a visit. The room with pink walls, two twin beds and posters of Caribbean artists on the wall always brought back a ton of memories. Good ones. She loved growing up in the Caribbean, and especially the Eleuthera Islands. It was a place where people were genuine. You could leave your front door open at night and not have to worry about being vandalized. Not like the States, or the other islands for that matter—where crime was prevalent. People slept with guns beneath their pillows.

She changed into a pair of boy-cut shorts and a gray T-shirt with Pink written across the front. She slipped beneath the covers on one of the twin beds and rested her head against the soft pillow. She grabbed her phone. Checked her email and then logged into Twitter. Sent a tweet and then logged into her Facebook account—scrolled along her timeline to see what had been posted. Her phone chimed when she received a text message. Lane.

Are you asleep?

Not quite.

You didn't say good-night.

You were busy.

Can we go for that walk on the beach?

Now?

Yes.

Okay. Meet you out front.

She sat up on the side of the bed. She slipped on a pair of shorts. Checked her face in the mirror and decided to dab a little eyeliner on her eyes. Popped a breath mint into her mouth and then slipped out of the room, down the hall and then slowly eased the front door open. Lane stood out front waiting for her.

"Hi, stranger," he said.

"Are you enjoying yourself?" She tilted her head to the side, smiled.

"I am. Your brothers are cool. And so is your pops."

"I'm glad you like them. And they like you," she said. "They make everyone feel like family."

"Wow, what a way to burst my bubble. I thought I was special."

"You are." She laughed and then led the way down the road toward the ocean.

She was surprised when Lane grabbed her hand, intertwined his fingers with hers.

"I'm sorry about them badgering you earlier. Getting all in your business. Those Talbots can be nosy sometimes."

"It's okay. They're just looking out for you."

"Yeah, I've never brought anyone home. Not for a long time."

"I see," said Lane. "Well, now I feel special."

"Good!" She took her flip-flops off when they reached the sand.

"It's so beautiful here," he said. "Again, I can't believe you left this place."

"I had to go find my way, my place in the world. Higher education was never an option for us, always a requirement. Except for my brother Denny, who opted for the military instead."

"So I heard. He told me all about it. And your brother Nate told me all about his art career in Atlanta, and Edward told me about his political career in Florida. And your father told me what it was like growing up in Key

West." Lane smiled. "I feel like I've known them all forever."

"Sounds like it."

"Made me feel closer to you." He stopped walking and pulled her close.

She rested her head against his chest, felt his heartbeat—breathed in his scent. She turned her head, placed her chin against his chest and looked into his eyes. He leaned down and before she could protest, his lips were already against hers and his tongue already probing the inside of her mouth. His fingertips began to caress her ample breasts. She should've stopped him. It was too soon for him to touch her in places that sent chills to her spine like that. Instead she caressed his strong chest.

He plopped down into the sand and pulled her down with him. Kneeling, her knees rested between his legs for a moment. He lay on his back and she found herself on top of him, straddling him. Her eyes closed tightly, he kissed her with intensity, hungrily. She'd never been kissed like that. She could feel him rising between her legs. She moaned. He sent her hormones into a whirlwind. His hands crept underneath her shirt, loosened her bra.

She pushed away from him. Stood. Breathing heavily, she said, "Too much. Too fast."

Eyes glazed, he rested upon his elbows. "Sorry."

"No apology necessary. It's just…"

"I know."

She fastened her bra and fixed her disheveled hair. Reached her hand out to help him up from the sand. Instead he pulled her back down, and she sat in between his legs, faced the ocean. He wrapped his arms tightly around her, rested his chin on top of her head. The waves made a tune as they crashed against the shore. As the moon rested against the dark sky, they talked about first loves and first kisses and laughed about family. The connection between them was undeniable.

A full two hours later, Whitney found it difficult to hold her eyes open.

"Let me get you home," he whispered.

She shook her head *yes*. "Long flight. Long day."

"When you're ready, I'm going to make sweet love to you. Like you've never been loved before."

Judging from the way her body had reacted only hours before, she believed him. No need denying that truth or challenging it. She would lose for sure.

Chapter 14

Whitney flipped hotcakes over a heated stove. Placed them on a platter. A set of earbuds in her ears, she moved her hips in a fast circular motion, engaging her body in a very sexy dance. Lane leaned against the doorpost, watching—a slight grin in the corner of his mouth. She had no idea he was there, and he liked it that way. The girl had rhythm, he thought, and a set of hips that he loved to watch.

She turned and saw him there. She jumped! He'd startled her. She pulled the earbuds from her ears.

"What are you doing?"

"Watching you." He grinned wider. "Just pretend I'm not here."

She sighed and shook her head. "You shouldn't sneak up on people like that, you know."

"I didn't sneak."

"You should've made your presence known." She smiled. "Are you hungry?"

"Starving." He said it seductively. There was a new sexual energy between them. One that wasn't there before.

"I mean for food."

"Yes, that, too," he said with a grin.

"Well, have a seat."

He pulled a chair from the kitchen table, sat down and rested his elbows on the table. Watched as Whitney loaded bacon, eggs and hotcakes onto a plate, placed it in front of him. She made herself a plate and set it opposite his.

"Looks good," he said.

"Eat up. We have a long day ahead of us."

"What are we doing?"

"We're going to start with shopping. Then I'm going to show you around the island a bit. We'll go jet-skiing and maybe have a bite to eat at one of the eateries on Harbour Island. I want to show you the Grove, our family's B and B. If all goes well, we'll be spending the night there."

"Nice."

"My brother's reception will be there tonight." Whitney sat across from him at the table. "We'll both be too intoxicated to make the long journey back to Governor's Harbour, so we'll just stay there."

"So you've already peeked into our future and know that we'll be intoxicated. Fascinating."

"Yes," she said. "But don't tell my mother. She wants us to stay here. Doesn't understand that I need some alone time."

"So you want to be alone with me?" he asked.

She sighed. Smiled. "Eat your food."

* * *

Whitney maneuvered her father's pickup down Queen's Highway, pointing out every landmark that Lane might be interested in knowing about. She showed him her old high school and her family's church. After stocking up on souvenirs at the gift shop, she'd managed to talk him into an early lunch on Harbour Island. He placed sunglasses on his face, rolled his window down and breathed in the beautiful island air.

She parked her father's truck at the boat dock, and they took the water taxi over to Harbour Island. The two of them snagged a high-top table on the patio at the restaurant, Queen Conch. Whitney sipped on a glass of ice water, while Lane gave the menu a look over.

"What do you recommend?"

"What do you like?"

"Anything seafood," said Lane.

"Are you open to trying new things?" She smiled.

"Somewhat."

"Try the conch salad."

"Conch?" he asked with a frown.

"It's a shellfish commonly eaten here in the Bahamas," she explained. "You had it in the fritters at dinner last night."

"Okay, I'll try it." He hoped he didn't regret his order. After all, he was a meat-and-potatoes type of guy, a full two hundred seventy-five pounds with a hearty appetite.

"Maybe you should order the grouper fish, as well."

"I will." He gave her a smile that had nothing to do with food. "I've enjoyed my trip so far. Thanks for inviting me."

"I'm glad. And no thanks necessary," she said. "You needed a vacation. You appear to be a workaholic."

"I'm not a workaholic," he challenged.

"When was the last time you took a vacation? I mean, like a real one—where you hopped on a plane and went somewhere."

"It's been a while. I haven't even been home to Saint Louis in a long time."

"Why haven't you gone home to visit your mum?"

"Long story."

"I have time," said Whitney.

"A lot of sad memories in that place. Ever since my brother died, it hasn't been the same," he said.

"What happened to your brother? Was he sick?"

"A car accident. We were both way too drunk, and neither of us should've been driving. But he insisted. And ended up dead, and here I am reliving it every single day of my life."

Whitney grabbed his hands. Held them tightly. "It's not your fault, you know."

"Had I not been intoxicated, I'd have made a rational decision. I would never have let him behind that wheel." Tears welled in his eyes, but he fought them with every inch of his being. He wouldn't let her see him cry. He changed the subject. It was enough talk of Tye and that dreadful night. He lived it enough in his dreams; he didn't need to live it while awake, too. "I have promised myself that I'm going home soon, though."

"I'm sure your mother misses that beautiful face of yours," she said. "Don't make her feel as if she's lost two sons."

Lane hung his head. His mother had told him the same thing the last time he spoke with her.

"You're right," he said and then quickly changed the subject from talk of Tye and his mother and home. "What are you having to eat?"

"The fritters." She smiled softly. "And don't disregard my comment."

"I didn't." He laughed a little. How did this woman know him so well? He looked her square in the eyes. "I said you were right."

"I have friends who have lost their mothers. Don't take yours for granted." She took another sip of her water. "Just sayin'."

She was right. He knew it.

Several rum punches later, the two took the water taxi back.

"Are you able to drive? You've been drinking, and I don't like the thought of that one bit."

"I haven't had nearly as much as you think."

He wouldn't relive his nightmare again. He would drive himself, but he'd never driven in the Bahamas and driving on the opposite side of the road was an intimidating thought.

"Are you sure? Maybe we can take a taxi and pick up your father's truck later."

"I'm fine. I swear."

He gave in but promised himself that the moment she looked out of control, she was pulling the truck over and calling for a taxi. Whitney drove her father's truck back to her parents' home without incident. They had a short time to dress and prepare for Edward's reception. Lane wasn't happy about having to wear a suit, but he'd get over it. After all, he wouldn't have to wear it for long.

He made his way to the guest bedroom where he'd spent the night before. Pulled his navy suit out of the closet and laid it across the bed. He pulled his shoes out of his bag and gave them a quick shine. Sat on the edge of the bed. Thoughts of Whitney swirled in his head.

He was feeling something for the woman who seemed to know him too well. He was comfortable with her—the girl-next-door type of comfortable.

After a quick shower, he was suited and smelling like Kenneth Cole's Black cologne. He took one last glimpse in the mirror before heading for the living room to wait for Whitney.

"Well, don't you look handsome," said Beverly Talbot.

"Thank you." He gave her a smile. "You look lovely, too."

She was dressed in a navy dress with lace. Lane took note of how beautiful the middle-aged woman was and wondered if Whitney would look like her when she was older. They shared the same smile and eyes.

"You're too sweet," said Beverly. "Would you like a drink?"

"Yes, ma'am."

"I'm having sky juice."

He followed her to the kitchen, where she prepared him a drink with gin and coconut milk. He wasn't much of a gin drinker, so he sipped slowly. But he wanted to be sociable and try new things, as Whitney had suggested earlier.

"Hello, son. You look nice," said Paul John as he entered the kitchen and slapped Lane on the back. "You clean up well."

Lane chuckled, thinking he must've looked pretty bad if Mr. Talbot thought he cleaned up well.

He smiled and said, "Thank you, sir."

"Mother, have you seen my black slacks?" asked Denny in a panic.

"You're not dressed yet?" Beverly frowned at her son. "What have you been doing all this time?"

"Looking for my slacks!" exclaimed Denny as he rushed out of the kitchen in a panic.

"He's been playing video games all day. What is he, twelve?" Nate asked to no one in particular as he entered the room. "Lane, nice suit."

"Thanks," said Lane as he sipped his sky juice.

"I see my mother has introduced you to her tonic," he said. "Careful, it creeps up on you."

"Okay."

"And where's the diva?" asked Nate, grabbing a Bahamian beer from the refrigerator.

"The diva is right here," said Whitney as she entered the kitchen wearing a short silver body-con dress that hugged every inch of her figure. The low-cut front revealed cleavage.

Lane was captivated. "Wow," he said.

Her eyes met his. "Look at you! All handsome and stuff."

"Dapper, huh?" He smiled.

"Very."

"That dress is pretty short," Nate commented. "Mum, you see how short this dress is? Is that appropriate for a wedding reception? You should go change."

"Shut up!" exclaimed Whitney and slapped her hand against her brother's chest.

"Do you wear this stuff in front of your kindergarten class at school?"

"I'm not at school, and my children aren't here," said Whitney. "And where is Denny? We're riding with him."

"Looking for his trousers."

"Jeez!" said Whitney. "Maybe we'll take a cab to the water taxi."

"Nobody's taking a cab anywhere," said Paul John. "I'll drive you two to the water taxi while Denny gets dressed."

Chapter 15

Her family's property, the Grove, was breathtaking—three historical beachfront properties on Harbour Island converted into beautiful bed-and-breakfasts. Each had its own distinct personality, theme and name. The Talbot House had flair and spunk and boasted bright colors. The Clydesdale had a musical ambiance, where portraits of jazz and Caribbean music legends adorned the walls, with a baby grand piano in the Grand Room. Decorated in tropical Caribbean colors, Samson Place was the most tranquil of the three.

Edward and Savannah's reception was to be held at the Clydesdale. It was the house where the family hosted their parties and special events. Lane and Whitney stepped inside the Grand Room of the Clydesdale. People had started to gather. Some of them sipped on cocktails and nibbled on hors d'oeuvres while chattering. Caribbean music played softly.

"Come on, I'll show you around." Whitney grabbed Lane's hand, intertwined her fingers with his and led him through the colorful home.

She peeked her head into the kitchen and whispered, "Raquel."

Raquel was the Grove's cook. But she was more than that. She'd been a friend of the Talbot family for years. She'd helped Beverly Talbot with the children when they were small. Whitney had been especially fond of Raquel. She'd been her confidante when she was a young girl.

"Hey, baby!" said the round woman with a caramel face. "When did you get here?"

"Yesterday." Whitney grinned. "Sneak me a couple of those conch fritters."

"You haven't changed one bit," said Raquel as she glanced over Whitney's shoulder with a smile. "And who do we have here?"

"This is Lane. Lane this is our very famous cook, Raquel. She makes the best Caribbean meals on the island."

"She's exaggerating," said Raquel and reached her hand out to Lane. "So nice to meet you."

"You, as well."

"He's cute," she tried whispering to Whitney. "You two make a cute couple."

Lane smiled at the compliment.

Whitney quickly interjected, "We're not a couple. Just friends. It's his first time in the Bahamas."

"I see," said Raquel thoughtfully. A grin danced in the corner of her mouth.

"So what about those conch fritters?" Whitney reminded her.

"You are a piece of work." Raquel grabbed Whitney's hand and led her deeper into the kitchen. "Lane, we'll be right back, honey."

"I'll be here waiting," he said.

They stood at the silver stove and Whitney grabbed three conch fritters and placed them in a napkin, wrapped them tightly.

"You've never brought a guy to the islands," said Raquel. "Not even…"

"I know," said Whitney. "There's a first time for everything. Besides, I didn't want to come home without a cutie on my arm."

"You like him?"

"He's okay. We're just getting to know each other."

"Does he have everything on that silly Man Menu of yours?"

"Not everything," said Whitney. "Shoot, not even most things."

"There's no perfect man out there, you know," said Raquel as she escorted Whitney back to the door of her kitchen. "You'd be surprised who you fall in love with."

"Well, there's no love here. And I don't believe in marriage or commitment. All three are overrated and worthless. People aren't faithful." She thought of her friend Kenya and the news she would have to share as soon as she returned to the States.

"Don't compartmentalize everything, baby."

"I'm not. Let me just say it's not for me," said Whitney. "I'm happy."

"Are you?"

"Absolutely!"

"Well, that makes me happy…if you're happy," said Raquel with a look of skepticism on her face.

"No worries." Whitney gave her a tight squeeze. "Thanks for the fritters."

"Always," said Raquel as she watched the couple walk away and head toward the bar. "So good to see you, baby. I'm glad you're home."

Whitney turned, blew her a kiss and then led the way to the patio. She slid onto a bar stool and Lane sat next to her.

"What are you drinking?" she asked.

Lane turned to the bartender. "You have some Skyy Vodka back there?" he asked.

"Yes, sir," said the bartender.

"Vodka and cranberry, then," he said.

"And for you, my lady?"

"A Merlot," said Whitney.

"What?" asked Lane. "Not a rum punch."

Did he know her that well?

"I like to sip on a glass of wine from time to time."

"I see."

His eyes met hers and stayed there. They were locked, and she felt something deep in the pit of her stomach. She wanted to break the stare but couldn't. He smiled, and she smiled back. He touched her chin with his fingertip. She wanted to kiss him at that moment and had no idea why—and certainly didn't want him to know it.

"One vodka cranberry." The bartender interrupted whatever moment they were having. "And one Merlot for the lady."

"Thank you," said Whitney, now looking at the bartender and taking a sip of her wine.

Lane glanced at the television mounted behind the bar. Checked the score of the football game. He pulled a folded piece of paper from his pants pocket. Studied it. She wanted to ask what it was but sipped her wine instead.

"Yes!" he exclaimed after the team scored a touchdown. "If they can pull this game off, I'll win three hundred dollars."

"Oh, those are wagers," she stated.

He was a gambler. Did he have an addiction or was this something he did for fun?

"Yeah, I do a little betting."

"I see."

He wanted to explain, she could tell. But he chose not to—just carefully slipped the paper back into his pocket, grabbed his drink and took a long sip.

"You're a gambler." It was more of a statement than a question.

"I'm not a gambler, but I do engage in a harmless wager from time to time."

"How often?" she asked.

"Enough. I like a good wager." His grin was entrancing.

"You sure it's not a habit?"

"I don't lie or beat around the bush. I keep it real." He became defensive.

She believed him. He seemed like the straight-up guy he proclaimed to be.

"Don't get all bent out of shape. I was just asking," she said.

"I don't have anything to hide."

"I bet your team doesn't win."

"I bet it does," he retorted.

She slammed a Bahamian bill on the bar. "I bet you five dollars."

"I can't spend Bahamian money in the States."

"You can spend it here…in the Bahamas."

"Okay, five dollars says my team wins. And I raise you."

"What?"

"My team wins and I get the five dollars, plus I get to finish what I started last night at the beach. What *we* started last night…"

"You're insane." She lowered her voice to a whisper. "Are you bribing me for sex?"

"It's called a wager."

"Wager, huh?"

"You wanted it just as much as I did," he said.

She did. There was no denying that, so she simply smiled. She turned her head and took a sip of her Merlot. "Okay, you're on."

Had she just gambled her body away?

On the dance floor, Lane had moves. Whitney loved to dance and was impressed that he was able to keep up. She shook her hips as they danced to the Caribbean tune. He grabbed her waist and the two moved in a rhythm of their own. Though the room was filled with friends and family celebrating Edward and Savannah's nuptials, it felt as if they were the only two people in the room. Whitney laughed. She couldn't remember the last time she'd had so much fun.

She'd already removed her heels long before. As the music slowed and Beres Hammond crooned from the deejay's huge speakers, Lane pulled her close—aggressively. She gave him a look that said *What do you think you're doing?* But part of her loved the aggression. She secretly appreciated how he handled her. His strong arms wrapped tightly around her and she rested her head against his chest. It felt as if she belonged there, in his arms. As if she'd known him forever. She raised her head and looked at him. He stared back.

She was going to enjoy losing that bet.

Chapter 16

He thought she was sexy as she stood in front of him. The provocative, transparent nightie clung to her hips and revealed her flesh—plump brown breasts and every inch of her brown hips, thighs and curves.

"Nice," he said.

"Nice?" she teased. "That's all you have to say about it?"

"Very nice," he replied.

He reclined in the high-back chair in the corner of the room. Sexy Caribbean music played on her iPhone. She moved to the music and danced her way over to him. She awakened his senses in every possible way, but he remained calm. He'd learned to hide his feelings and show no anxiety about things. The key was to never get too excited. That way you were never disappointed.

When she reached him, she continued to move her hips to the music in front of him. He reached for her hips, caressed them underneath the nightie. He grabbed her bare ass and pulled her closer between his legs. He felt himself rise beneath his slacks. As much as he tried to control everything around him, he couldn't control that. She turned him on. His heart beat rapidly.

She straddled his lap and moved her face closer to his—kissed his lips, slowly and passionately. He removed the straps of the lingerie from her shoulders, caressed her breasts and squeezed her nipples. Moved his hands to the rhythm of the music before leaning in; took one of her breasts into his mouth. He alternated between sucking and licking each of her mounds. He stood, lifted her and carried her to the bed. Her brown legs wrapped around his waist, he gently placed her onto the bed. Removed his shirt, trousers and then peeled his boxer shorts off. He pulled a condom from the pocket of his slacks.

He planted kisses along the inside of her thighs and then worked his way to the center of her sweetness. His tongue danced there and she moaned. She grabbed his head, stroked his scalp. He stayed there until her legs shook and she begged him to stop. The mischievous part of him continued despite her plea.

Finally, he freed her from his grip, moved onto the bed and hovered over her. Kissed her lips slowly, passionately. His tongue danced with hers, and her chest moved up and down as she breathed heavily. He placed himself inside her warmth and she moaned. He moved to the rhythm of the music. He kissed her lips, nose and forehead. Her hips rose to meet his. He'd lost control, something he didn't do very often. But this woman caused him anxiety every single time he encountered her. And now he was certainly at her mercy.

He squeezed her tightly and unleashed every emotion he'd felt since the moment he saw her.

He collapsed onto his back on the bed next to her. He was spent. He looked over at her and gave her a warm smile, pulled her close. No words were necessary. He let the words of the song that played, "Fight This Feeling," serenade them and say all that he wanted to say. When he looked at her again, her eyes were lightly closed. A light smile danced in the corner of her mouth.

He loved the Bahamas, the night and everything about it all.

The sunlight crept into the room as he struggled to open his eyes. Completely naked and uncovered, he looked around trying to remember where he was. He looked over at the empty spot next to him on the bed. She was already up and about, he thought. Thoughts of Whitney filled his mind. When he heard someone turning the handle on the door, he pulled the crisp white sheet up to his waist and placed his arms above his head.

"Wake up, sleepyhead," said the beautiful woman who had seduced him the night before.

She was dressed in a white sundress and carrying a tray of food.

"I'm awake," he said.

"I didn't know what you liked, so I brought a little of everything."

"I don't usually eat breakfast."

"It's the most important meal of the day." She recited the line, and he suspected she said it often to her students.

He sat up and leaned his back against the headboard. She placed the tray onto his lap, and he took a sip of orange juice. Took a bite of wheat toast.

"Looks good."

"Raquel prepared it especially for you."

"I must thank her."

"You must." She smiled. "What do you want to do today?"

"Can we just stay here all day and do what we did last night?"

"I would love to—" she crawled onto the bed, leaned in and kissed his lips "—but my parents are expecting us for dinner later."

"Until then?"

Whitney laughed. "Okay, until then."

They took the water taxi back to the Eleuthera Islands. Paul John waited for them at the boat dock. They hopped into the old pickup truck—Whitney slid into the middle next to her father, and Lane slid in close to her. He slammed the door and placed a pair of shades onto his face. The wind blew against his face as they drove down Queen's Highway toward Governor's Harbour and back to Whitney's childhood home.

Beverly Talbot met him with another glass of sky juice.

"He doesn't drink gin, Mother," said Whitney as she eyed him from across the room. "He drinks vodka."

"It's okay. I like it," he said. Even though he wasn't a gin drinker, he took it. It was his way of connecting with her mother.

"He said he likes it." Beverly Talbot smiled at her daughter. "Now make yourself useful. Go to the kitchen and check on the macaroni and cheese."

Whitney pouted for a moment but did as her mother instructed. Beverly escorted Lane to the living room, where Caribbean music played on an old stereo.

"Have a seat, son," said Beverly.

"Yes, ma'am." He took a seat on the love seat.

Beverly took a seat across the room from him. "My daughter has never brought anyone home, you know."

"Really?" he asked casually.

"I was starting to think she didn't like men at all," said Beverly. "But I really think she's just afraid of commitment. And afraid of love."

The conversation made Lane uncomfortable, mainly because those were his fears she'd just described.

"Fear is very real," he said and took a sip of his drink.

"Don't tell me you're afraid, too," said Beverly.

"I've been known to be cautious."

"But you like my daughter?" She smiled.

"Beverly, can I see you for a moment?" Paul John stepped into the living room and beckoned for his prying wife.

"Right now?"

"Right now," Paul John said.

Beverly stood. Reluctantly. "I'll be right back, son."

Paul John grabbed her elbow and ushered her out of the room. Lane heard Whitney's father gently admonishing his wife about her questions. He pretended not to hear, but a slight grin danced in the corner of his mouth.

"What's so funny?" Whitney asked as she returned to the room.

"Your mom was giving me the third degree and your father rescued me."

"That sounds like him. Always rescuing someone." Whitney smiled and shook her head. "You enjoying your sky juice?"

"Not really," Lane admitted.

"You don't have to drink it." Whitney took the glass

out of his hand and took it into the kitchen. "I'll bring you a beer."

As she walked out of the room, Lane watched as her hips swayed from side to side. Thoughts of their love-making swarmed in his head. He wanted her again, imagined all of the things he would do to her once they were alone again. She must've felt him watching, because she turned and looked at him before disappearing into the kitchen. She was back just as quickly with that beer; handed it to him.

"Thank you." Soon the rest of Whitney's siblings began to fill the house. And the family spent the evening enjoying a Bahamian feast—baked fish, fried chicken, Bahamian macaroni and cheese, collard greens and johnnycakes. They drank, laughed and talked about the days of growing up on the island. And when the sun began to set, the family gathered in the living room and sang together.

Lane hadn't experienced family time quite like that, but it made his heart feel good. He felt closer to Whitney than he had when they first arrived on the island. He entertained the idea of opening his heart to a woman—something he hadn't done in quite some time. He was feeling something. He wasn't sure that it was *love*, necessarily, but it was definitely something.

Chapter 17

It had been three days. Three whole days since they'd returned from the Bahamas and three whole days since she'd heard from him. She had rested her head on his chest the entire flight home. His cologne had filled her nostrils for five hours. He held her hand as they stood at baggage claim waiting for their luggage to show up on the belt. They had taken an Uber to her home, and he'd spent the night—his strong arms wrapped around her through the night. He'd showered and gone home early that morning. Promised to call her after he'd gotten settled in and recovered from their long trip.

That was Monday. Here it was Wednesday afternoon, and she was ushering her kindergarten class to their buses. She kept a smile on her face for the sake of her five- and six-year-olds, but inside, she was dying. Dying to know what she'd said or done to run Lane away. She'd left him two voice messages and texted three times.

He's an asshole, she thought. She couldn't believe that she had let her guard down, left her heart wide-open. It was her own fault. After she'd ushered her children to their buses, she went back to her classroom and retrieved her things. She felt deflated as she sat behind the wheel of her car. Reminisced about the beautiful moments they'd shared in the Bahamas—the lovemaking, the walks on the beach, the time with her family. She was sure they'd connected. She revisited every conversation they'd had. Perhaps she'd said something, done something. She couldn't think of one single thing that would make a man lose interest after a weekend such as the one they'd just shared.

She was tired of thinking about it. Wouldn't give it any more of her energy. She dialed Kenya's phone number, pulled out of the school's parking lot.

"So I see you've decided to return to the States?" Kenya asked.

"Got back on Sunday."

"And I'm just now hearing from you?"

"It's been a busy few days, just trying to get back into the swing of things."

"What's that I hear in your voice?"

"Nothing," Whitney lied.

"Come on, Whit. I know you."

"Let's have a drink."

Loud conversations filled the room, and a live band played a variety of instruments—drums, bass guitar and keyboard. The vocalist sang an old Frankie Beverly number.

Kenya shook her hips before taking a seat at their cozy corner table. "I love this group!"

"They are good." Whitney slipped her purse into the empty chair against the wall.

"A nice way to break up the work week, right?"

"Yes. It's a nice atmosphere. And the band is amazing," said Whitney. "How did you find this place?"

"It's been here for years. It's like a historical landmark or something. The owner is well-known in the community and it's been in his family for generations. Lots of local bands got their start here, and when celebrities roll through town, they come here for, like, their after-hours set," said Kenya. "He's selling the place, though. Can't afford to keep the doors open."

"Wow, it's sad he has to sell the place. Sounds like a wonderful family legacy."

"I know, it is sad."

"I hope he sells to someone who will love it and keep the history alive."

Kenya leaned in and whispered, "Will owns this plaza. The owner pays him rent."

"Really?" Whitney cringed at the mention of Will's name.

"But the owner is in trouble, and Will is hoping that he walks away from the place. He wants to turn it into one of those upscale places. Cater to a certain clientele—you know, the ones who have lots of money to spend," said Kenya. "He says it's why Max is in the trouble he's in now, because he caters to a low-budget clientele."

A male server appeared at their table. "What can I get you ladies to drink?"

"Rum and pineapple for me." Whitney pulled a small compact from her purse, checked her hair.

"I'll have a Merlot—" Kenya gave the server a smile "—and a glass of water."

"Great, I'll be right back with your drinks." The server disappeared.

"So what's going on with you, girl? You know I can read you like a book." Kenya leaned back in her chair, crossed her leg. "Don't tell me, the truck driver wasn't all he was cracked up to be?"

"Actually, we had a great time. An amazing time, really. My family loved him—" Whitney rolled her eyes "—especially my mother."

"Oh my God! Mama Talbot loved him?"

"She gave him the third degree that she gives everyone. And Daddy gets along with everyone." Whitney lowered her voice. "We even...you know..."

"Shut. Up. You slept with him?" Kenya asked.

"Shhh! Don't tell everyone."

"You bad girl." Kenya grinned wickedly. "Give me details. Was he an amateur or pro?"

"It was very nice."

"Then I'm confused. What's the problem?"

"I haven't heard from him since he left my place on Sunday," said Whitney. "I've left text messages and voice messages. Am I expecting too much?"

"Hell no! You gave up the goods." Kenya smiled before noticing that Whitney wasn't smiling. "How often did you talk before you left for the Bahamas?"

"Every day. Sometimes several times throughout the day."

"And nothing since you returned?"

"Not a peep. And it's driving me crazy trying to figure out what I said or did wrong."

"Screw him!" Kenya exclaimed. "If he's not going to give you the courtesy of an explanation, then so be it! Move on. He doesn't deserve you."

Whitney shook her head in agreement. "You're right."

Whitney hoped that Kenya would be able to dismiss Will so easily.

"You like him!" Kenya peered at her friend. "You haven't fallen in love, have you?"

"No!" Whitney lied. "Girl, no."

"You're such a liar. You love him!"

Whitney sighed heavily. Turned toward the band. "I haven't had time to analyze what it is I'm feeling."

"Have you forgotten about your Man Menu?"

"No."

"Does he even meet a third of the criteria?"

"I haven't forgotten the Man Menu." Whitney avoided the question. "Now let's change the subject. We're here to unwind, right?"

"Right." Kenya gave her a look of skepticism.

The server placed drinks in front of them. Whitney smiled and bounced her head to the music. She checked her phone for missed calls or messages. There were several, but not one from Lane.

"Be right back. Going to the little girls' room." Kenya stood. "If that server comes back, tell him to bring me some hot wings."

Whitney chuckled. "Will do."

She watched as Kenya made her way across the room and then glanced over at the bar. There he was, standing there. He looked up at the television mounted on the wall, his arms folded across his chest. Well, at least he wasn't dead, she thought. The nerve of him standing there like everything was fine. She wanted to go to him, confront him. Give him her wrath. But when a soft caramel arm appeared out of nowhere and locked arms with his and a woman rested her head against his shoulder, she decided against it. She struggled to catch her breath, and her heart sank into the pit of her stomach. She'd been replaced by a woman in a short blue dress.

He whispered something in her ear. With that, he began bidding a farewell to everyone at the bar. He laughed about something that the bartender said and then turned to the woman, ushered her toward a table on the other side of the room.

Whitney had allowed herself to be vulnerable, and for that she blamed herself. She'd been so careful about guarding her heart and not letting anyone in. It was her way of protecting herself. Yet she'd gone against her own rules, and now here she was—angry. She had no right to be angry. He wasn't hers in the first place.

Kenya was right, she thought. He didn't deserve her.

Chapter 18

The Bahamas had been mind-blowing. He'd needed a vacation, and it had exceeded his expectations by far. Not to mention the beautiful woman who had been his companion. She'd had his emotions so off balance that he needed a few days to analyze what was going on. So many times he'd picked up the phone to call or text but couldn't. Then on top of it, work had been beyond busy—his hours had been insane. He'd fallen asleep on the sofa two nights in a row, and without supper.

Whitney had left a few messages, and he fully intended to return them, but between recuperating, working and sorting through his feelings, he hadn't gotten around to it. He'd have gone home and passed out on the couch tonight, but his cousin Nicole had shown up on his doorstep and insisted that he take her out for a drink.

"It's my birthday! Are you going to force me to celebrate alone?" she'd begged. "Just one drink, dude."

"What about your girlfriends? Wouldn't you rather hang out with one of them?"

"Come on, Lane. Put some clothes on!" she said, then went to his kitchen and swung his refrigerator open. Made herself at home.

"What about your little boyfriend—the one I met at Christmastime?"

"He's history," she said and poured a glass of fruit punch. "Let's go have a drink at Max's."

Lane sighed. "Just one drink. That's it. I have to get up for work at three o'clock."

"In the morning?"

"In the morning."

"One drink, I promise." She grinned.

In the car, Nicole had inquired about Whitney. "Tell me about this woman you went to the Bahamas with. You like her?"

"She's okay," said Lane nonchalantly, a slight grin in the corner of his mouth.

"You like her. Look at your face."

"What's wrong with my face?"

"You have that look," she pointed out. "You went to a whole other country with her! Did you meet her family?"

"Yep."

"You met her family?" Nicole smiled, turned toward him in her seat. "Oh my goodness! That's serious, dude."

"Not at all."

"Are you doing that thing again?"

"What thing?"

"That thing where you get scared and run from love. Are you going to let Helena ruin your life forever?"

"She's not ruining anything."

"Then why are you running from this woman who you clearly have a thing for?"

"What makes you think I have a thing for her?"

"You barely take time off from work to go to the doctor. Yet you take an entire week's vacation to go to the Bahamas with a woman…you meet her family. You come back with this grin on your face…"

"It wasn't a week. It was just a couple of days." Lane smiled. "And what grin?"

"That one!" Nicole exclaimed. "All I'm going to say is, if you like her and she likes you, then why not go for it? Don't mess it up like you did before. Don't let her get away, Lane. Give love a chance. It doesn't come along that often."

"Nobody's in love." That was all he said before pulling into the parking lot at Max's.

"Fine. Stay in denial." Nicole stepped out of the car. "When she hooks up with some other guy, don't come crying to me. I'm just gonna say 'I told you so.'"

"Shut your door so I can lock the car," he said, ignoring her last comment. It affected him, though—her comment. The thought of Whitney with another man bothered him a little bit.

She flicked her tongue out and then headed for Max's. He followed and held the door open for her. The loud music greeted them the moment they walked in. Lane headed straight for the bar. It was his routine. The bar was where all of the regulars hung out, and sometimes he'd catch Max behind the bar working if it was a busy night. He usually greeted Max before snagging a seat.

"My man," said Max as he walked up. He was dressed

in a blue suit and actually floating around greeting his clientele, as an owner should.

The two shook hands.

"I thought you'd be slaving behind the bar," said Lane.

"Not tonight. We're fully staffed."

"Hey, Max," said Nicole with a smile.

"Hi, sweetheart." Max gave Nicole a strong hug. "You're looking gorgeous as ever."

"Thank you."

"How did you get this old fellow out of the house in the middle of the week?"

"It's my birthday! And it wasn't easy."

"Well, now. Happy birthday!" exclaimed Max. "Your first drink is on the house."

Nicole hugged Max again, kissed his cheek. "You're a sweetie."

Lane stood at the bar, looked up at the television mounted on the wall. He wanted to catch the score.

Nicole looped her arm inside his and rested her head against his shoulder. "Thank you for coming out with me tonight, cuzzo. We won't stay out long, I promise. I know you have to work."

"It's cool. Glad I could celebrate with you." Lane grinned. "Especially since you don't have any other friends."

"Shut up." She pushed away. "I have friends. I just wanted to hang with my favorite cousin."

"Well, good."

"Now…about those free drinks."

"*Drinks?* Max said one drink," said Lane.

"Well, you're going to treat me to the others," Nicole laughed.

Lane shook his head and stared at the screen.

Max walked up, patted Lane on the back. "I have your table ready."

Max escorted them to their table across the room. Nicole excused herself, went to the ladies' room.

"Have you given my offer any more thought?" asked Max.

"About taking over the business," Lane said matter-of-factly. "It's all I've been thinking about."

"And?"

"I think we should schedule some time to talk about it. Have a real conversation," said Lane. "I'm definitely interested."

"Good." Max exhaled. "I'll set something up."

He couldn't wait to get Nicole back to her car at the end of the night. He needed to make a phone call—a private one. He knew that Whitney had early mornings and didn't want to call her too late, but he needed to call before the night was over. He couldn't believe he'd been so foolish, not returning her calls and text messages. How was he going to explain his actions? He hoped she would forgive him.

Chapter 19

Whitney stepped out of the shower, wrapped a thick towel around her body. She'd cleansed and moisturized her face, rubbed coconut oil all over it. Glanced in the mirror. Her thoughts drifted to Lane and the woman in blue. She shook her head, wished she hadn't allowed her heart to be so vulnerable. She'd usually been so guarded, yet she'd let her guard down for once.

"Stupid," she whispered to herself as she grabbed a tube of lotion from the bathroom sink, plopped down on the side of her bed.

When her phone rang, she searched for it in the bottom of her purse. She looked at the screen. *Lane.* The nerve of him, she thought. Had he managed to find a moment to call her after he'd dropped his date off? She rejected the call. He called right back. She rejected the call again. When her phone chimed, she knew he'd left her a text message. However, she wasn't interested in anything he had to say. Instead of reading it, she began to massage lotion into her mocha-colored skin. She slipped into a pair of boy pajama pants and pulled a T-shirt over her head.

Curiosity got the best of her and she grabbed her phone. Read the text message.

Hello, Whitney. I'm sorry to call so late. Also sorry for not calling in a few days. I've been sorting through some things. I hope you're still talking to me.

She tossed the phone against the pillow as she slipped beneath the covers. She reached over and turned off the lamp on her nightstand. She didn't need Lane, or his apologies. She had moved on.

Her five- and six-year-olds seemed busier and more playful than usual. She had asked them three times to make a single-file line in the hallway. She rarely had to repeat herself with her class, but today was different. Maybe her patience was thinner than it had been on other days. She closed her eyes for a brief moment and then asked them again.

"Please form a single-file line along the wall, people, if you want to eat lunch today," she said. "Is anybody hungry?"

They all raised their miniature hands and then did as they were told. She led the way to the cafeteria, where her students took their places at their assigned table. She enjoyed the lunch hour. It was the only time of the day that she got a real break from her class. She slipped back down the hallway to her classroom, where her packed lunch—a ham sandwich and a small bag of Doritos—awaited her return.

When she turned the corner, she noticed her class-room door was ajar. She could've sworn she'd locked it. She wasn't careless that way. She pushed the door and walked in and was startled to see Paula, the assistant principal, and Bridgette, the office secretary, chatting with Lane. The three of them laughed like old friends.

"Here she is," said Paula.

She wanted to check her hair and lipstick to make sure she was presentable, but there was no time for that. He stood there dressed in tan khakis, work boots and black T-shirt. A green bandanna was wrapped around his head. She should've been mortified, but she couldn't help noticing how handsome he looked, even in his work attire. She wondered what he was doing there in the middle of the day, but as soon as she heard the thunder and saw a bolt of lightning flash across the classroom window, she quickly remembered he didn't work in the rain. A smile crept into the corner of her mouth when she saw the dozen white roses in a vase resting on her desk.

"Hello," she said.

"Lane was just telling us about your trip to the Bahamas!" Bridgette exclaimed. "It sounds so beautiful over there!"

"I thought he should leave your roses on your desk, instead of in the office. Besides, he insisted," said Paula. "No harm, right?"

"Not at all. Thank you, Paula," said Whitney.

Paula gave Lane a smile before exiting the room. "Pleasure meeting you, Mr. Martin."

"Pleasure was all mine, Paula," said Lane. "And great meeting you, too, Bridgette."

Bridgette shook his hand like a groupie would shake the hand of a celebrity. Whitney didn't know how she felt about him being so damn charming. Once they were alone, she sat on the edge of her desk, thinking of how she was going to read him! How dare he show up at her school unannounced, and after being too chummy with that woman at Max's. And insist that her assistant principal let him into her classroom. She would have a conversation with Paula about that.

"I'm sorry," he said, a look of sincerity on his face. "I was wrong."

"Yes, you were," was all she could muster before he approached her.

He wrapped his arms around her waist. "You forgive me?"

How could she not with those beautiful brown eyes staring into hers?

"Forgive you for what?" she asked. What was he referring to?

"For not calling when we returned to the States."

"And the woman you were with?" she asked. "Not that I care. And you don't owe me an explanation. We're not in a relationship or anything."

"What woman?"

"It's not a big deal. Forget I mentioned it."

"What *woman*?" he asked again.

"Last night, at Max's."

He thought for a moment. "Oh, you mean my cousin?"

Was he seriously going to use the *cousin* excuse?

"Yeah…your cousin." She said it sarcastically, a smile in the corner of her mouth. She shook her head.

"Yes, I was with my cousin Nicole at Max's last night. It was her birthday and she insisted that I take her out for a drink," he said. "Not that I owe you an explanation or anything."

"You're right."

"So you were at Max's," he said emphatically.

"Yes."

"And you didn't bother to say hello."

"You were busy."

"Not for you."

"Apparently so."

"Were you alone?"

"With Kenya."

"How do I know that? Maybe you were tucked away in the corner with some guy."

"I went there after work for a drink with Kenya. Spilling my guts about how I had this incredible time in the Bahamas with a guy that I really like, and we get back to the States and I don't hear a peep from him!"

"So you like me?"

"That's totally beyond the point."

"I was an asshole." He moved closer, grabbed her by the waist.

"Such an asshole."

"But you forgive me."

"I don't," she lied. She'd forgiven him the moment she saw his beautiful face in her classroom. "I don't forgive you. I'm done. And when I say I'm done, I really mean it."

"You mean it?" he asked, his lips grazing her neck.

Her breathing increased. Something always happened to her emotions when he got close.

"I mean it," she whispered.

His hand touched the small of her back, massaged it. His lips touched hers, and he kissed her. "I'm sorry," he whispered.

"I can't...forgive you..."

His lips covered hers. When the bell rang for the students to return to class, she knew she needed to break free from his embrace, but she struggled. Her hormones were already stirred.

"I know your students will be here in a moment." He kissed her nose. "Have dinner with me later."

"I'm still mad," she said.

"Mad people still have to eat."

She knew she should play hard to get, teach him a lesson. She usually didn't let men off the hook so easily. One strike and they were out of the game—and out of her life. But this was different. She felt herself crumbling, and she didn't like it one bit. It had been a long time since she'd felt what she was feeling for this guy who was all wrong for her. But she couldn't control it. She was a woman who was always in control, yet every second she was in his presence she was losing it.

"I'll pick you up at eight."

"Fine," she heard her voice say.

She watched as he left and her kindergarten class pounded into the room.

She didn't have much time to analyze her feelings. After a long afternoon, she had a small window to get home, shower and get dressed for dinner. She decided to wear something sexy, though she hadn't a clue about where he was taking her. She chose the red dress that she'd purchased her last trip to New York with Kenya and Tasha. The spaghetti straps were the only things covering her shoulders. She put silver earrings in her ears and stepped into a pair of strappy sexy heels. She heard the doorbell just as she dabbed her neck with perfume.

She rushed to the front door and peeped out. Lane stood on her doorstep. He'd changed into a pair of jeans and an old Mizzou T-shirt. She wondered if their signals had been crossed. She thought about how he had mentioned dinner. And dinner in her book meant that he'd be taking her someplace nice—not another sports bar like the one they'd gone to on their first date. She felt disappointed. He was definitely not in her league, she thought.

She swung the door open and immediately felt overdressed.

"Wow," he said. "You look beautiful."

"I guess I should've asked how I should dress."

"I think you nailed it."

"I feel overdressed. Maybe I should change."

"I think you look perfect. Just live in the moment for a change. You spend too much time trying to make sure things are this way or that. Just enjoy the space you're in right now. You look beautiful… Who cares if it's the appropriate attire."

She grabbed her purse from the kitchen counter. "Okay," she said.

He held the door open and she hopped into the cab of his pickup. Slid into the passenger's seat and pulled the seat belt around her waist. Hip-hop music blared from his speakers as he pulled out of her subdivision.

"Sorry, this is my song," he said and turned the volume up.

"Lil Wayne?" she asked in a judgmental tone.

"Yes. You have a problem with Lil Wayne?"

"So many. How much time do you have?" she said. "He curses too much, too many tattoos. Not to mention his outlook on life is somewhat warped. Just my opinion."

"What does that have to do with his music?"

"Are you even listening to the lyrics of this song?"

"No, I just like the beat. Makes me want to move in my seat. But if I had to think about him as a person, I admire his struggle. He had a poverty-stricken upbringing, much like mine," said Lane. "My mom was a single mother who raised three boys on her own."

"I bet it was hard for her."

"She refused to take any handouts after my pops walked out on us. And she made sure that every one of us went to college," he said. "Football was my saving grace. So when I look at Lil Wayne, I know that he's not much different from me. Just a young kid who found his way out through his talent—music."

"I guess that's a way of looking at it." She gazed out the window. Wondered where he was taking her.

When he finally pulled the truck into a parking lot, she sat up straight in her seat. The sign read Bachman Lake. He pulled into an available space.

"What are we doing here?" she asked.

He shut the engine off, hopped out of the truck and came around to open her door. He helped her out of the truck. "You'll see."

She followed him toward the lake. He held on to her as she attempted to walk across the grass in heels. She was grateful that the rain had cleared, yet the grass was still a bit damp. This was certainly not what she'd had in mind when he'd invited her to dine with him. She enjoyed surprises as much as the next person, but her patience was wearing thin. She felt his fingers intertwine with hers.

"Look at that sunset," he said. "Isn't it beautiful?"

It was, she thought. "Yes."

Then she saw it—a table in the middle of the grass, a crisp white tablecloth covering it, and a single red rose in a vase in the center of the table. A small speaker played Caribbean music, and the place setting for two was carefully arranged. A smile crept into the corner of her mouth. He walked over and pulled her chair out, held his hand out and beckoned her to have a seat. She sat down and he walked around to his chair across from her.

"I know you were probably expecting a lobster tail or juicy steak, but I'm afraid you'll have to settle for Rudy's Fried Chicken. The best fried chicken this side of Dallas."

She laughed. Fried chicken was not at all what she'd expected, but she was impressed by his ingenuity.

"I've never had Rudy's."

"What?" he asked. "How long have you lived in Dallas?"

"Long enough."

"Well, obviously you've been sheltered, so let's bring you up to speed," said Lane.

"And you pulled all of this together by yourself?"

"No, I had a coconspirator."

She recognized the young lady from Max's as she walked toward them from the parking lot. "I forgot the wine," she said. "Had to run back and grab it."

"Whitney, this is my cousin Nicole. Nicole, Whitney."

"Pleased to meet you, Whitney. I've heard a lot about you."

"Pleased to meet you, too."

Nicole pulled two wineglasses from her huge purse, placed one in front of each of them and poured.

"Thanks, Nicole," said Lane.

"You owe me, big-time," she tried whispering, but Whitney heard her.

"I took you out for drinks last night," said Lane. "And on a work night, too."

"Yes, you did—" she lowered her voice to a whisper "—but the line at Rudy's was wrapped around the building!"

"It always is," said Lane. "Thank you for going the extra mile."

"I'm just glad to see you step out of your box for a change. Man!" She turned to Whitney. "He never does anything like this for anyone. I think he really likes you."

"That will be all, Nicole. Thank you," Lane interrupted.

"He's a really great guy," Nicole continued. "A workaholic, and really stubborn sometimes…but a great guy. I hope you'll give him a second chance."

"Nicole, really?"

"I'm going!" said Nicole. "It was very nice meeting you, Whitney."

"Very nice meeting you, Nicole," said Whitney as she giggled.

Nicole walked away. Whitney and Lane locked eyes.

"She was sweet," said Whitney.

"You weren't thinking that last night," joked Lane.

"You're right. I wasn't. But this…this is all very nice, and thoughtful."

"Thank you."

"So what is it that you needed to sort through?" she asked.

"I don't know. The Bahamas had my emotions stirred. I wasn't sure what it was I was feeling when I returned. And I certainly don't want to hurt you."

"Hurt me how?"

"I'm no good at relationships. I work a lot, my hours are crazy, I like to be alone sometimes..."

"I work a lot and I like my alone time, too. Love my girl time."

"I just felt like the next step was a commitment and I wasn't sure that's what I wanted."

"We don't have to decide any of that right away. What's wrong with taking our time?"

"Nothing," he said.

"We should let things happen at their own pace."

"I'm cool with that."

"But we have to be respectful of each other and return calls and text messages. Even if we're feeling unsure about things," she warned.

"I'm sorry."

"And as long as we keep the lines of communication open and discuss stuff..."

"I'm okay with that," said Lane. "I had a wonderful time in the Bahamas. You have an awesome family."

"Thank you. I like them, too."

"I appreciate you inviting me. I never do anything like that."

"You're welcome."

"I don't know where this is going, but I would like to continue seeing you. Every chance I get."

"Me, too." She smiled.

She took a sip of her wine and felt content. Though it wasn't a fancy restaurant with hors d'oeuvres and the like, it had to be the best dinner she'd had in a very, very long time.

Chapter 20

She'd long kicked her shoes off and sat across from him on the sofa, waving her arms in the air, trying to get her point across. They'd talked politics and relationships, world issues and religion for three hours straight. Lane glanced at the clock on the wall for the first time and watched as the hands approached two o'clock. He'd lost track of time, and the liquor didn't help. The more they drank, the more they talked. He yawned. His workweek had caught up with him.

"You're sleepy," she said. "I've worn out my welcome."

"No! I've really enjoyed talking to you."

"Is it almost two already?" she asked.

"That it is."

"I'm sorry." She stood. "You should drive me home."

"I don't think either of us should drive like this," he

stated. "The last thing we need is to get into an accident or get stopped by the cops."

"I'm just a little tipsy."

"You should stay. It's Friday night, so neither of us has to work in the morning."

Lane had become quite comfortable with Whitney. He hadn't met anyone in a long time that he wanted more than a roll in the hay with. The women he met— some of them were desperate, many of them gold diggers looking for a man to take care of them. None of them held his attention for any length of time. However, after meeting Whitney, he actually entertained the thought of a future with a woman. She was easy to be with and even easier to talk to. He shared things with her, things he hadn't shared with anyone, old wounds he hadn't opened in years. Sharing with her made his demons seem less scary.

He'd told her all about Lane Jr. and what an incredible athlete he was, but telling her wasn't quite the same as her seeing it in person. She needed to see him play and judge for herself.

"Lane Jr. has a game in the morning. I would love for you to come."

"Are you sure?"

"I'm sure. You need to see how good he is out there. He's dominating the football field. Just like his old dad used to do."

"I'm sure he is, but do you think my coming to his game is such a good idea?"

"I think it's a great idea."

"I want to make sure it's healthy for him. For us."

"Can you stop being an educator for a moment. It's just a football game, sweetheart."

"Okay." Whitney giggled. "I'll go."

"Good." He stood. "I have two guest bedrooms. You can take either one that you want. Or you're welcome to sleep in my bedroom, with me. I won't touch you, unless you want me to."

"Okay. I'll take one of the guest rooms."

"Okay. Feel free to make yourself at home. The bathroom is down the hall." He pointed toward the bathroom. "And there's my room in case you need anything."

"Great."

She chose the middle bedroom and Lane was grateful because he'd recently placed fresh sheets on the bed. He flipped on the light for her and handed her the remote control for the television.

"Do you need an extra blanket?"

"No, I think I'll be fine."

"If you need anything, I'm right in here."

"Okay, good night," she said.

"Good night."

Lane was completely exhausted and knew that sleep would find him the moment his head hit the pillow. He went into his bedroom, changed into a pair of shorts and an old T-shirt. He left the door ajar in case Whitney needed anything. He sat on the side of the bed and unlocked his phone. Sent a text.

You ready?

Yea dad, I'm ready.

How did practice go?

It was okay. Coach was hard today.

Listen to your coach.

I will.

Ok, good night, son. I'll see you tomorrow.

Gn dad.

He shut his phone and crawled beneath the covers. He turned off the bedside lamp. He was exhausted but suddenly not so sleepy. His phone jingled. A text message.

Are you asleep yet?

He smiled when he read Whitney's text.

It's only been five minutes.

I miss you already.

He turned the bedside light back on. Got up and went to the guest bedroom. Whitney was curled up beneath the covers. He could see her shadow in the darkness. He didn't bother to turn on the light, just crawled into the queen-size bed next to her. Wrapped his arms tightly around her waist. She felt good there, like she belonged in his arms. She snuggled against him. Before long he could hear light snores escaping from her mouth. He smiled. She would never believe him if he told her she snored, for real this time. So he'd keep it to himself. Soon his eyes were too heavy to remain open, and he gave in to the sleep.

On Saturday morning, Lane Jr. was on the field warming up. Soon he glanced across the field and gave his father a wave. Lane waved back. His ex-wife, Helena, followed her son's eyes and spotted Lane in the bleachers. He gave her a smile and a wave. She didn't smile back, just waved and then instantly locked her eyes on Whitney. She watched as they took their seats and then adjusted in hers so that her back was to them. He'd learned long ago that the best way to deal with her was to kill her with kindness. She would never get another opportunity to hurt him.

Lane Jr. always played like a polished athlete. Lane was on his best behavior. He was learning to control his temper during the game so he wouldn't get thrown from the field again. Being ejected didn't feel good and didn't provide the best example for his son. He knew that Lane Jr. wouldn't be very receptive to Whitney at first—he'd always had hopes of his parents reuniting, but Lane was confident that if he gave her a chance, he'd become fond of her, too. He hoped, anyway.

All he said when he met her was "Hey."

"That was quite a game you played out there, young man," said Whitney.

"Thanks."

"You work on that pass a little bit, and you'd be flawless."

Lane Jr. shrugged. "That's what my coach says."

"It's what your dad says, too," said Lane.

Most women doted over Lane Jr., but Whitney had a way with him that let him know that she didn't care that he was a star football player. She was used to dealing with kids his age. Lane respected that. He was falling for her.

"Come on, honey, grab your things. Let's go," Helena interrupted. "Tell your dad goodbye."

"Bye, Dad. I'll see you next weekend."

"We'll go check out that movie you've been wanting to see," said Lane. "The sci-fi one."

"Okay, that's cool."

"Say goodbye to Miss Whitney," Lane reminded him.

"Goodbye," said Lane Jr. "Nice meeting you."

"Nice meeting you, too."

Lane grabbed Whitney's hand and the two walked to his car. He opened her door and she stepped in. He hopped into the driver's seat, started the engine and sat there for a moment. He turned the volume down on the radio. He moved his body so that he was facing her.

"What's up, babe?" she asked. It was the first time she'd called him by an endearing name.

"I think I'm ready to go home for a visit."

"Really?"

"Yes. But only if you'll go with me."

"I don't know, Lane. I just took off for the Bahamas. I don't know if I can get the time off."

"We'll make it a quick turnaround. A weekend."

When his mother insisted that he come home to Saint Louis for a visit, Lane knew that he couldn't run from the pain of his past any longer. Fear had kept him away for a long time, but Whitney had given him courage again. He felt empowered when she was around. Lane knew that his mother would love her. She was the girl that every mother wanted for her son—beautiful, smart, respectful and someone who cared for him. With her Bahamian accent and quirky sense of humor, she would quickly win over his entire family.

"Okay," she surrendered. "When?"

"Next weekend."

She sighed, took a deep breath. "Okay."

He smiled and leaned over and kissed her lips.
"Thank you, babe."

He exhaled.

Chapter 21

Whitney was falling for Lane. He made her feel as no one ever had. She finally felt that tingle in the pit of her stomach that she'd only heard talk of. But he was the wrong guy—wasn't he? Her friends certainly would think so. Kenya would give him the benefit of the doubt, but Tasha would be beside herself with judgment. So she hid him. He would be her little secret.

In the Bahamas, they had connected. She wasn't surprised at all that her family had fallen in love with him. They didn't care what he did for a living or that he'd been previously divorced and had a teenage son. Those had been her hang-ups in the beginning. However, she hadn't given any of that a second thought when they made love at the Grove beneath the Caribbean moonlight. And it certainly didn't matter now. She was all in.

As the wheels of the jet hit the pavement, Lane held on tightly to her hand. He kissed the back of it.

"We're here," he said.

"Yes, we are."

She knew he hadn't been home since his brother Tye's funeral. That had to be weighing heavy on him. Her heart went out to him. She wished she could take away the pain and the fear. That was the thing that validated her love for him. She wanted nothing more than to see him happy. But grief was a terrible thief. It always managed to steal hope, happiness and joy from people—without warning and without mercy.

"My brother Clint is picking us up at the airport."

"Can't wait to meet him."

"He'll love you."

They deplaned and headed straight for baggage claim. A man who was an older version of Lane, with a tattered salt-and-pepper beard, stood near the carousel. A wide smile covered his face when he saw them. Lane went straight for him. They slapped hands and hugged strongly.

"My little brother!" said the man. He patted Lane's stomach. "What you been eating?"

"The same thing you've been eating," said Lane as he returned the pat to his brother's stomach. He grabbed Clint's beard. "And this bird's nest of yours is out of control. You need to shave, man!"

"The ladies love my beard!" said Clint.

They both laughed, heartily and without regard for where they were.

"Come here, babe." Lane grabbed her by the hand. "This is Whitney. Whitney, my brother Clint."

"Pleased to meet you, Clint."

"Is he holding you hostage, young lady?" Clint playfully asked. "Because if he is, I'd be happy to rescue a pretty lady like you."

"Watch it, bro. This is my woman!"

She was stunned by his words. When did she become his woman? They'd just had a discussion about relationships and commitments, but suddenly she had a title. She wasn't quite sure how she felt about that title and she'd address it with him later.

"Pleased to meet you, Clint. I've heard a lot about you."

"I haven't heard anything about you," said Clint as he took her hand in his and gave her a quick scan from head to toe. "What are you doing slumming with this guy?"

"He's a sweetheart," said Whitney.

"Oh, what a beautiful accent."

"She's from the islands."

"Very nice dialect," said Clint. He owned a beautiful smile quite similar to Lane's. She could definitely tell they were brothers. "Let's get these bags. Your mother is beside herself with excitement. Cooked all this food… all of your favorite stuff. She never cooks like that for me!"

"It's because you live here. She doesn't see me every day, so she has to make up for lost time."

"Lost time, my ass! She cooked enough food to feed an army. Got everybody coming over tonight for a crab boil, like you're a celebrity or something."

"Don't hate…appreciate…"

Whitney enjoyed the playful banter between Lane and his brother. It was a side of him she hadn't seen. The men grabbed their bags from the carousel and they trampled out to the parking lot to Clint's car.

"Mama's still driving this old Chrysler?" asked Lane.

"Yeah, man. She's going to drive it until the wheels fall off. You just watch."

They threw luggage into the trunk of the old Chrysler. Whitney slid into the front seat of the car, with the worn red leather seats and wood-grain dashboard. Lane hopped into the back seat. Clint started the car and pulled out of the parking lot, music blaring from Saint Louis's hip-hop station. He sang every word to every song along the way, in between updating Lane on everything that had taken place since he'd been gone. Clint also pointed out every landmark that he thought Whitney might be interested in seeing—the Saint Louis Arch, Sweetie Pie's soul food restaurant and Busch Stadium.

Finally, they pulled up in front of Lane's childhood home—an old two-story traditional brick house with a large front porch. A slender woman of average height stepped onto the porch with a cigarette extending from her long fingers.

"I thought she stopped smoking!" Lane frowned and gazed at his young-looking mother.

"She did for a while. Now she's back at it."

"I'll take care of that," Lane said matter-of-factly as he hopped out of the back seat of the car.

He opened Whitney's door and then rushed to the front porch. He grabbed his mother into his arms and lifted her into the air. She laughed with exuberance. She couldn't contain the joy of seeing her son.

"Well, if it isn't the prodigal child," she said and grabbed his face into both her hands. "How are you, baby?"

"I'm good, Ma."

"You look so good! I have missed you like crazy."

"I've missed you, too."

"And who do we have here?" She looked past Lane and saw Whitney climbing the porch steps.

"This is Whitney. Whitney, my mother, Sylvia."

"Pleased to meet you." Whitney smiled at Lane's young-looking mother, with dark brown flawless skin like Lane's. They were twins, she thought.

"Nice to meet you, honey. I know you must be something special, because my son doesn't bring women home," said Sylvia. "Come on in here and get something to eat. I know you two must be hungry."

The house smelled of seafood and Cajun spices. They followed Sylvia to the kitchen, with the glass table and four chairs and a vase with fresh flowers. A large aluminum crawfish pot stood tall atop the gas stove. Sylvia walked over and stirred whatever was in it.

Lane took a sniff in the pot. "Seafood boil."

"You like seafood, Whitney?" asked Sylvia.

"Yes, ma'am," said Whitney. "Love it. It's the staple of my home."

"Which is where?"

"The Bahamas."

"Ahh, the Bahamas! I've always wanted to go there."

"It's beautiful, Ma. You would love it."

"You mean you've been to the Bahamas?"

"Yes, ma'am, a few weeks ago."

"Okay, so what's really going on here?" asked a skeptical Sylvia.

Lane kissed her cheek. "Don't know what you're talking about."

"Mmm-hmm." Sylvia pointed toward the cabinets above the sink. "Grab a couple of bowls from the shelf over there, honey."

Whitney was standing closest to the shelf and grabbed two bowls, handed them to Sylvia. She filled each of them with shrimp, crab legs, fish, corn and potatoes.

"Have a seat and enjoy. I have to go get your rooms ready," said Sylvia. She kissed the top of Lane's head and wrapped her arms around his neck. "When I come back, we'll catch up."

She disappeared from the kitchen.

"Notice she said *rooms*. Plural." Lane laughed.

"Just like my mother. You don't sleep together unless you're married. Otherwise you burn in hell."

"No worries." Lane lowered his voice to a whisper. "I'll just sneak in your room after the lights go out."

"I don't think so."

"You don't want me to sneak in your room and rock you to sleep?"

"You're not getting me in trouble with your mother. I have to make a good impression."

"She'll never know. She sleeps like a rock."

"Not taking any chances."

"We'll see." He grinned and took a mouthful of seafood.

Before long the house was crowded with Lane's uncles, aunts and cousins. His aunts brought dishes filled with food—red beans and rice, fried fish, cakes and pies. They were all excited to see Lane and he them. Loud music and louder voices filled the house. Bottles of rum, vodka and tequila filled the dining room table. A game of dominoes was being played at a card table. Lane had long found his home at the table and slammed dominoes down. He taunted his cousin and claimed that he was the "king of dominoes." Surely it was the vodka talking, Whitney thought. She smiled at him, and he gave her a wink of the eye. He was enjoying himself immensely and it warmed her heart. She didn't understand how he could stay away from this bunch of people for so long. Their love for him was undeniable.

Lane's mother pulled up a chair next to hers. She leaned over toward Whitney. "He looks happy. I haven't seen him happy in a long time, even before Tye's death. He was always so serious."

"Really?"

"And then after the accident, I thought he wouldn't recover. I thought I wouldn't recover. It was the hardest thing I'd ever had to endure."

"I'm so sorry."

"I was watching *Queen Sugar* one night, and Remy said to Charley, 'You can't outrun grief… It leaves when it's ready. Sit with it, listen to it, respect it.' Those words were so profound. Helped me out a lot," she said. "You watch that show?"

"Yes, ma'am, I've seen a couple of episodes," said Whitney.

"I tell you, that Ralph Angel is something to look at, ain't he?" Sylvia laughed.

Whitney laughed. "He's a good-looking guy."

"I love that the show is set in Louisiana. That's where my family's from."

"Lane told me. Says we're going to drive down there sometime."

"That's good. I'm glad my family is close to him. So even when he can't make it home, he can get to them."

"Yes, there's nothing like family."

"You're absolutely right," said Sylvia. She stood. "I'm going to dance. You want to get out there and show us what you got?"

"No, ma'am, I'll sit this one out."

"Okay, baby." Sylvia joined her brother in the middle of the floor.

Whitney sipped on a glass of wine and chitchatted with Lane's aunts and female cousins. She discovered that his cousin Diana taught middle school, so she and Whitney had plenty to talk about. They hit it off right away, swapping classroom stories. His aunt Jean played the piano and wrote music. She encouraged Whitney to follow her passion for music. Before long, she felt as if she knew every one of them intimately. She already loved them.

"I hear Lane's going to visit Tye's grave site tomorrow," said Aunt Jean.

"Yes," said Whitney.

"He's never been there. It'll be hard on him."

"But you'll be there with him, right?" asked Diana.

"Yes, I will. I'll be right by his side," said Whitney.

"Good." Aunt Jean gave her the warmest smile. "He's lucky to have you."

Sylvia was in the middle of the living room floor dancing with Lane's uncle Bud. She swung her hips from side to side while the Marvin Gaye track played, a glass of wine in her hand. She was in her element, happy that her son was home. Whitney smiled.

"Come over here, Whitney, and dance. Show me how they do it in the islands."

Whitney's heart dropped. Was she serious?

"Come on, child, before the song ends!"

Whitney stood and gave Lane a look of despair.

He smiled and raised his glass in the air. "Go show 'em what you got, baby," he yelled.

He was no help whatsoever, she thought as she made her way to the living room, where Sylvia was dancing. She moved to the music. She loved to dance, and she was good at it. However, she hadn't planned on dancing in front of Lane's entire family, whom she'd met only hours before. However, by the time the song changed, she was all in. She ended up dancing the night away.

After every guest had been bid a good night, Whitney helped Sylvia put food in plastic containers and placed them in the refrigerator. Sylvia's eyes were tired. She looked like a woman who was at least ten years younger than she really was—fit and energetic—but her eyes told a different story. Whitney could tell that years of being a single parent and experiencing heartache had worn on her. Whitney had been raised in a two-parent home with six children and she knew that parenting was no easy task. Her heart went out to Sylvia.

"You make my son smile," she said. "Are you two serious?"

Things had grown rather quickly in the past few weeks, and Whitney hadn't had a moment to analyze what she and Lane were or weren't. She'd only lived in the moment. Usually she lied to herself or the people around her. However, she needed to be honest with this woman who'd endured enough in her life.

"I like him." Whitney smiled. "I actually think that I'm falling for him."

It was the first time she'd admitted it or said it aloud.

"Well, he's definitely fallen for you," said Sylvia. "What do you two plan to do about it?"

"Just live in the moment. I don't think that either of us is looking for a commitment."

"It's funny how we always seem to find what we're not looking for." Sylvia gave Whitney a strong hug. "Thank you, honey. You go on up and I'll see you in the morning."

"Good night."

When she passed Lane's bedroom, she could literally hear him snoring loudly. She smiled and shook her head. She loved that he knew exactly how to be himself, without inhibition or shame. He didn't care what people thought or said. He was simply who he was, and after meeting his mother, Sylvia, she knew exactly where he'd gotten it from. He had threatened to sneak into her room, but she was sure he wouldn't be sneaking into anyone's room before the night was over. She crawled into bed in the guest bedroom, with bedding that smelled of lavender fabric softener. A jasmine candle rested on the nightstand. She rested her head against the pillow and tried giving in to sleep, but as she stared at the ceiling, she knew that rest wouldn't come easy.

Chapter 22

The drive to the cemetery seemed like the longest drive ever. Lane glanced over at Whitney in the passenger's seat as she held on to a bouquet of artificial roses. He grabbed her hand and held it tightly. He was grateful that she was making this drive with him. He didn't know if he could've done it alone.

"Thank you," he said.

"You'll be fine."

"I know."

He drove his mother's Chrysler across the gravel road and then slowed and parked at the place where his brother's grave was located. He stepped out of the car and then came around and opened Whitney's door, grabbed her hand and helped her out of the car. They searched for Tye's headstone. It was made of granite and engraved with his name and photo. He remembered that photo of Tye, and the moment he saw it, his heart ached and a tear crept down his cheek. He modestly wiped it away and then stood there with his arms folded across his chest. Whitney placed red roses atop the granite.

"I should never have let him behind the wheel."

"You both were intoxicated, and both very young. Allow yourself to be forgiven."

Those words made him cry, hard. His guilt was so strong he couldn't see his way to forgiveness. He'd robbed his mother of a son. He'd robbed Clint and himself of a brother. Whitney wrapped her arms tightly around his waist.

"He had so much going for him."

"What do you remember about Tye?"

Lane thought for a moment. "So much. So many childhood memories of us running up and down the block. He was a great athlete. He was funny, obnoxious at times. I remember some of the crazy things he used to do."

"Yeah?"

"Yeah. He also had a way with the ladies. And he was so smart. He had the best memory of anybody I know. In fact, he remembered things that I wished he would forget." Lane laughed at that memory.

"You will always have those memories. Nothing can ever take those away. That's what you hold on to. That's how you keep him alive in your heart."

"We can go now. I don't ever want to come back here again. I want to remember him living, not dead."

"Okay."

"I just needed to face my fears, once and for all," said Lane. "Let's go home."

"You sure? You've come a long way in order to say your goodbyes and make your peace."

"And I have," he said. "I also came to check on my

mom. See how she's doing. I abandoned her when she needed me most. Caught up in my own feelings. I want to just spend the last few hours I have with her until we leave for the airport. I know I need to get back here more often."

"That would surely make her happy, Lane. Please do that."

"Maybe I'll send for her and Clint to come see me in Texas. Well, she doesn't fly, but maybe I can drive up and get her."

"Maybe," said Whitney. "She would love it."

"She loves garage sales!" Lane laughed at the thought.

"So do I! You can find some great treasures at garage sales," said Whitney. "Maybe I could show her some of my favorite places."

"You would do that?"

"Absolutely!"

Lane pulled Whitney into him, wrapped his arms tightly around her. His lips engulfed hers in a passionate kiss. Where had she been all of his life?

His mother had fried chicken, mashed potatoes, collard greens and corn bread prepared for them when they returned to the house. She'd even skipped church just to have a few extra minutes with them before they were whisked off to Saint Louis Lambert International Airport. The visit was short, but much had been accomplished. Lane had managed to conquer his fears a bit and was even on the road to releasing himself from guilt. It was a process, but at least he'd made the first step.

"Do you feel like you got closure?" Sylvia asked. She sat directly across from Lane at the dinner table.

"Somewhat," said Lane. "I'm working on it."

"That's good, son. We all miss Tye, but we have to move on with our lives. We can't stop living because he did, you know. And we have to make sure that we stay connected with each other. We're all we have."

"I know, Mama."

"Don't make me come to Texas and whip your natural-born ass."

Clint laughed heartily at his mother's comment.

"I'm sorry for not coming home sooner," said Lane as he stuffed mashed potatoes into his mouth. "I was just talking to Whitney about flying you and Clint down for a visit."

"Boy, you know I am not getting on anybody's airplane! If God wanted me to fly, he'd have given me wings."

Lane looked over at Whitney, who gave him a half smile.

"We'll be happy to come back and get you," said Whitney.

"Well, aren't you just the sweetest," said Sylvia and grabbed Whitney's hand and gave it a squeeze.

"What? That was my idea!" said Lane with a high-pitched voice. "I just told her that."

Whitney laughed.

"Oh, boy, stop whining so much," said Sylvia with a laugh.

"He's always been a whiner, Mama. You know that," Clint chimed in.

"Wow! She steals my idea and gets all the credit."

"Well, when should I expect this to take place? I'm a busy woman, you know. You have to give me advance notice."

"Ma, you're retired."

"Doesn't mean I don't have a life."

"She just wants to brag to the sisters at church that she's going on vacation," said Clint.

Lane laughed. "I'll check my vacation time at work and let you know when I can get away. Sometime within the next month or two."

"I'll be ready." Sylvia smiled. "I guess I need to go shopping."

"Use the account I have set up for you," said Lane. "Buy whatever you want."

"I think I will," said Sylvia.

They finished dinner and chatted about what they were going to do in Texas, and then Clint and Lane took bags to the car. The look on his mother's face broke his heart. He knew it was hard for her to watch him leave. She'd miss him. She'd had so much life while he was there; he hoped she wouldn't go back to grieving. He needed to make good on his promise of returning to Saint Louis, and he would. The trip home had empowered him.

By the time the flight had ascended into the air, Whitney was asleep. She rested her head against Lane's shoulder, and he placed his head against the top of hers. Life was good at that moment. When he returned to Dallas, he would search for a ring—a ruby or something—not just a regular old diamond. He'd done some research and discovered that ruby was her birthstone. And not an engagement ring, just a friendship one. Well, maybe a little more than friendship. Maybe a ring that said *I want to be more than friends, but not quite married.* There was no doubt in his mind that he loved this woman. He had come to that conclusion. Now he just needed to express it to her.

He stepped out of the shower and wrapped a thick towel around his waist. He brushed his teeth, while Whitney wrapped her arms around him from behind.

"What time do you go in tomorrow?"

"Two o'clock."

"Wow, can they make it any earlier?" She reached into the pocket of her robe, pulled out a key. "Here, take this. You can lock up in the morning when you leave so that I don't have to get up. I'll be deep into my dreams about that time."

He turned around and faced her. "You sure?"

"Of course. It's not a big deal. I'll get it back from you later."

He took the key and placed it on the bathroom sink. Went back to brushing his teeth as she removed her robe and stepped into the shower. When she walked into the bedroom, dry and naked, he was waiting for her. His body was stretched across her king-size bed, and he propped himself up on his elbow. He watched as she moved toward her nightie drawer.

"No need for that." He grinned. He grabbed her by the arm, pulled her onto the bed. "Come here."

She landed on top of him, her breasts pressed against his chest. He kissed her lips, and his tongue danced inside her mouth. He grabbed the roundness of her butt, and then his fingertips danced up and down her back. His lips abandoned hers and made their way to her plump breasts, inhaled each one. His tongue swirled around her nipples. He parted her thighs and then flipped her over onto her back. He planted gentle kisses along her neck, breasts and stomach. His fingers gently entered her, played with her, danced inside her. She moaned with desire.

"Yes," she whispered.

"You like that, baby?" he asked.

"So much." She shook with desire.

He entered her and made sweet love to the woman

he'd fallen for. She wrapped her arms tightly around his neck, and he knew that he wanted to make her feel this way forever.

Chapter 23

She was ready to tell her friends about him. She needed to tell someone about this man who didn't have all of the qualities on her Man Menu but who brought chills up and down her spine and made her toes curl. They needed to know that she was happy. That after years of running men away, she'd finally found one she wanted to stay.

She'd trusted him enough to give him a key to her home. And they were spending so much time together that he'd given her a key to his home, as well. They weren't moving in together but thought it necessary to have access to each other's lives and space. She'd become quite comfortable with him and decided to drop by his place after work to whip him up a nice Bahamian meal before he got home from his long, stressful day.

She rubbed Bahamian seasonings on the fish and placed it in the oven. She chopped fresh cabbage and placed it into a pot. She whipped up a pot of peas and rice and re-created her mother's johnnycakes. The smell in the house reminded her of home. She turned up the volume on her Caribbean playlist—allowed Tarrus Riley to tease her senses. She shook her hips Bahamian-style.

Her friends had been blowing up her phone since before she'd gone to Saint Louis. She felt it was time to finally catch up with them. She called them both on a three-way and placed them on speakerphone as she continued to prepare her island favorites.

"So we're glad to finally catch up with you," said Kenya. "I've been worried."

"I'm doing fine. No need to worry, Mother."

"Haven't talked to you since Max's. And we talk just about every day!"

"I know, honey. And I'm sorry. There's just been so much going on."

"I'll say!" exclaimed Tasha. "You've been quite busy."

"When are we going to meet him? You've already gone trampling to the Bahamas with him. And did I understand correctly? You've gone to his home in Saint Louis, too?" asked Kenya. She seemed betrayed. "But you haven't even introduced him to your besties."

"I will! I promise," said Whitney.

"Who is this guy? Is it Will's friend? The one who owns his own business?"

"It's not Will's friend," said Kenya. "She blew him off. It's the truck driver."

"Truck driver?" asked Tasha, and Whitney could just imagine that she had a turned-up nose. "Are you kidding?"

"What's wrong with that?" Whitney asked. "He's a hardworking, upstanding man."

"What kind of future is that for you, Whit?" asked Tasha. "Have you forgotten about our Man Menu? We don't date men who drives trucks."

"You must really like him, though," said Kenya, "because we haven't seen you in, like, forever."

"Does he have anything on your list?" Tasha asked. "At least eighty percent?"

Whitney was hesitant to respond. "He has some."

"What's his salary?" Tasha demanded.

"I don't know what his salary is...and I don't care."

She hadn't heard Lane walk into the house, and it was too late to stop her friends from completely humiliating him. She hoped that he'd missed most of Tasha's comments, but he hadn't. He'd heard it all.

"Look, ladies, I'm sorry, but I have to go," said Whitney.

"We're not done with you, sister," said Kenya.

"I promise we'll do dinner one day this week."

"Yeah, we'll finish this later," said Tasha. "My masseur is here, and he needs my full attention, but let's do dinner this week."

"Love you, Whit. We'll talk later," said Kenya.

"Okay," she said before hanging up.

Lane had retreated to his bedroom, pulled boots from his aching feet. He sat on the edge of the bed. His face held a frown. She stepped into his arms, but his embrace wasn't as strong as it normally was.

"I made you a nice Bahamian meal," she said cheerfully.

"Smells good," he said. "I'm going to hop into the shower."

"Lane!" she called as he left the room. "Don't pay any attention to them."

"You sure you don't want a guy who works for corporate America, a white-collar dude, with a six-figure salary?" he asked.

"I'm sure. I want you."

"I'm not what you want, Whitney," he told her. "You should move on."

"I don't want to move on. I want you."

"I really just want to be alone right now. I had a really hard day."

"Are you asking me to leave?"

"I guess I am."

"You're serious right now." It was more of a statement rather than a question.

"I'll catch up with you tomorrow."

"What about the food I just prepared?"

He shrugged.

Her heart was broken. He pushed past her and went into the bathroom to shower. She went into the kitchen, packed food into plastic dishes. She grabbed her wine that had been chilling in the refrigerator and left his place, frustrated. She started her car and sat there for a moment. Tears welled in her eyes and she allowed them to roll down her cheeks. Just when he'd finally made it past the friend zone, and when she'd finally had the courage to let someone in—all the way in—she regretted it. To finally give a relationship a chance at longevity, and here he was telling her to *move on*. Tears blurred her vision as she drove home. She told herself that she would never let her guard down again.

She sat in her kitchen and ate Bahamian food alone, washed it down with two glasses of Riesling. No music and the kitchen light was the only light in the house.

She ate in silence. Thought of calling or texting Lane, but he'd been very clear about her leaving. She would give him his space. He would come around. She placed dishes into the dishwasher and started it.

Started the shower. After showering, she lay in bed, stared at the ceiling. Wondered if Lane would at least call or text to say good-night. He always did. However, her phone didn't ring, nor was there a jingle that indicated she had a text message. She thought he was overreacting but would give him his space. Tomorrow was a new day. She turned off her bedside light and shut her eyes.

Chapter 24

His day had sucked. Every moment of it. He'd over-reacted. He realized it later. He'd let his frustrations from the job get the best of him. And it hadn't helped that Whitney's friends didn't think he was good enough for her. He regretted letting her walk out that door, but his ego had gotten the best of him, and since he had run into yet another incident at work, he was drowning in self-pity.

This time, his supervisor insisted that he terminate an employee, one who, in Lane's opinion, didn't warrant termination. Sure, Tyler was Melvin's nephew, but he was also a hard, upstanding worker. He'd proved himself in just a short time. He was one of his best guys. Recently his past had reared its ugly head, and he'd gotten pulled over and arrested for a warrant he hadn't had a chance to take care of. He'd told Lane about it a few days before, and Lane had promised to help him fix things.

After being bailed out of jail, Tyler had been tardy that morning. Lane preferred to give him a warning rather than terminate him, but his new supervisor insisted on termination. He found himself in a hard place. If he fired Tyler, he risked his friendship with Melvin. If he refused, he risked his own reprimand. Particularly since this was his third run-in with his first-line supervisor.

"If you won't do it, then I will," his first-line had insisted. "And you can enjoy a three-day suspension."

"I won't fire him. He's one of my best guys."

"He was late again. The second time in less than thirty days, and if you haven't forgotten, he's still on probation."

"He had a good excuse for being late."

"Doesn't matter."

"I won't fire him. I'll give him a warning. Third time, and I'll let him go."

"No! You'll let him go this time."

"I won't," said Lane. "Do what you gotta do."

"Fine. You're suspended for three days. You can pack up and go home."

He'd been suspended for standing up for what was right. He removed his hard hat and vest and packed his things, threw them into the bed of his truck. He started his truck, turned the Lil Wayne track up as loud as it would go and then peeled out of the parking lot. He would fight the suspension, but he was so angry he saw red. Couldn't wait to contact the owner of the company and plead his case. But in the meantime, he needed to figure out how to make up three days' worth of pay.

Whitney had already texted that she was headed to his place and that she'd be preparing a meal. Before this happened, he was excited about spending the evening with her. However, on the drive home, he'd changed his mind. Wanted to be alone and wallow in his despair. And when he'd heard the comments of Whitney's uppity friends on the phone, he admitted, he'd lost his head.

She deserved someone else, he thought. Someone more refined or sophisticated. Someone who had more than a few qualities on her so-called Man Menu. Who was he fooling, thinking that he was good enough? He was a truck driver with baggage and emotional issues. There were guys out there who were a better fit. And if he weren't in the way, she might be able to find them. He decided that he would give her the space to do exactly that.

He stretched out on the sofa, something he hadn't done in weeks. Since Whitney had come into his life, she had him actually sleeping in his bed. She packed him healthy lunches and prepared dinner on days he was too tired to prepare it for himself. He'd gone from eating bowls of cereal and ice cream for dinner to eating healthy Bahamian meals. He'd even seen a change in his waistline. He would certainly miss those things, but being a bachelor wasn't so bad.

He watched college basketball until his eyelids were too heavy to stay open.

The second day on that couch and he was bored out of his wits. He pointed the remote at the television and surfed the channels looking for sports. His phone rang and he hoped it was Whitney. He had called her twice and texted, but she hadn't returned his calls or text message. They were both as stubborn as mules, one not willing to give in to the other. But it was better this way. She should go her way, and he his. The last thing he wanted to do was hurt her. And he didn't want her settling for someone who didn't meet her standards.

The owner of the company was finally returning his call.

"Hello, Lane. Sorry it took me so long to get back with you," said Perry. "I heard what went on, and let me just say that I've spoken with Blake. He was wrong for suspending you."

"Yes, he was," said Lane.

"I can't do anything about your friend that was fired, but I want you to return to work tomorrow. And you'll get paid for today."

"Thanks, Perry, but I don't want to return as a supervisor. Not as long as Blake's in charge. I want my old job back."

"Man, you drive a hard bargain. I need that position filled," said Perry. "But I'll respect your wishes. You go back to your old position tomorrow."

"Good. Thank you."

That was good news. He felt bad that Tyler had lost his job, but at least he wasn't the one who'd had to fire him. And he was grateful to have his job back.

Chapter 25

She met Kenya and Tasha for dinner, although she wanted to be alone. She just wanted to sit at her baby grand and make music. It was what she did when she was feeling down. Music always changed her mood. It gave her strength. It was her passion. But Kenya insisted.

"You don't need to be sitting in the house sulking," she'd said. "That's not healthy."

"I'm fine. I'm over it."

"Well, good. But you still have to eat, right?"

"I guess I do."

"We'll meet you at our favorite place in downtown Dallas at seven. We're not taking no for an answer. We're worried about you."

"Fine," said Whitney.

She took a seat across the table from them. It looked as if this would be more of an interrogation than a dinner. Whitney gave the menu a quick glance. Nothing sounded good, but she decided on the turkey club and an Arnold Palmer.

"I'm sorry that Lane overheard us talking, sweetie. I never meant for this to hurt him," said Kenya.

"But we only spoke the truth," Tasha chimed in. "You're too good for him. If he doesn't live up to your standards, then what is the point?"

"The point is, I liked him regardless of the stupid Man Menu."

"Oh, it's stupid now? The Man Menu has been a part of our lives since college. We live by it. It keeps us grounded," said Tasha.

"Not every good guy is going to have every single thing on the Man Menu. And furthermore, we created it in college. We were young and dumb then. We're grown women now."

"I used the Man Menu to find my Louis."

"And I used it to find Will."

"And how's that working out for you two?" said Whitney.

"What's that supposed to mean?" said Tasha.

Whitney was in a mood and decided to toss pleasantries out the window. "It means that you both ended up with men who met all of the criteria on the Man Menu but are cheaters."

"Excuse me?" asked Tasha with plenty of attitude.

"Louis fathered a child outside of your marriage." She looked Tasha square in the eyes. "Did the Man Menu prevent that from happening? Hmm?"

"How dare you?" asked Tasha. "I told you both that in confidence, because you were my friends. Not for you to throw it up in my face."

"But it's true."

"And I'll have you know that Will is not a cheater. He's a workaholic, but a cheater he is not!" said Kenya in defense of her fiancé.

"Are you sure about that?"

"What's that supposed to mean, Whit?" asked Kenya.

"Why should I say it? You won't believe me anyway. It'll be just like when we were in college."

"If you have something to say, just say it!" she exclaimed.

"I saw Will a few weeks ago. He was with another woman, kissing her in public, and in broad daylight," said Whitney as she took a sip of her Arnold Palmer. "I was in my car. He was so engrossed in what he was doing, he didn't even see me."

"I can't believe you just said that to me!" Tears welled in Kenya's eyes.

Whitney immediately regretted her words. Wished she could take them back. She'd planned on telling Kenya about Will, but not like this. She wanted to do it in private, and with a lot more empathy.

"I'm sorry, Kenya," she said. "I didn't want to tell you like this."

"Well, how and when were you going to tell me? You've been holding on to this for a few weeks?"

"I didn't know how to tell you. I didn't think you would believe me."

"You just want to get me back for the things we said about Lane on the phone the other night. Want to make me feel the way you felt."

"I'm being honest right now. But if you must know the truth…yes, the things you two said about Lane were awful. Especially you, Tasha! I probably lost the only man that I've ever truly loved. The two of you were so busy judging me, you forgot to look in your own damn backyards and realize that your men aren't all that great." Whitney dug into her purse and pulled out a twenty-dollar bill.

"You love him?" Kenya asked genuinely.

Whitney didn't respond, just placed the money on the table. "That's for my food. I'm out of here."

She walked briskly out of the restaurant and to her car. She sat in the driver's seat for a moment, reflected on the last few moments of her life. Suddenly she felt alone. She lost not only Lane but quite possibly her two best friends, as well.

She walked into the quiet of her home and decided it should remain quiet. She didn't turn on the television or music, like she always did. Instead she tossed her keys on the kitchen counter and removed her shoes. She plopped down onto the sofa and grabbed her laptop, placed it in her lap. She logged into Facebook and realized that she had a message waiting in Messenger. She'd received a message from one of the local lounge owners she'd reached out to about performing one of her pieces. Sean Goldwin had replied that he wanted her to perform at the end of the month on a Friday night. He would pay her two hundred dollars, and if he liked her, they would discuss a regular gig. She replied yes and then shut down the computer.

She sat at her baby grand piano and flipped through her music notebook. She needed to find her best three songs and practice them like crazy. Despite the crazy week she'd just had, music always changed her mood. Her plan was to get lost in it and block out everything and everyone from the outside world. She turned her cell phone off and placed it on top of the piano. She didn't need any interference.

* * *

She remained disconnected for the next few days, leaving her cell phone off. She poured her all into her kindergarten class each day, and each night she poured an equal amount of energy into her music. She wanted to be well prepared for her debut. After she'd settled on her best three songs, she practiced until her eyelids wouldn't allow her to play anymore. She would certainly be ready.

When her doorbell rang, she looked at her watch. Seven thirty. She couldn't think of a single person who should be ringing her doorbell. She hadn't invited anyone over for a visit, and most people didn't just pop up unannounced. She walked over to the door and peeped out. *Kenya.* She continued pretending not to be home.

"I know you're in there, Whit. Open the door," said Kenya.

Whitney didn't respond, just sighed and swung the door open. She turned and walked away from the door and sat at her baby grand, flipped through her music notebook.

"I tried calling your phone," said Kenya. "It kept going straight to voice mail."

"I turned it off."

"I'm sorry, Whit. Sorry about all of this," said Kenya.

"Okay." Whitney dismissed her friend's apology, stared at her music notebook.

She began to play a song, drowning out any further conversation. She hoped Kenya would get frustrated and leave.

"Whitney!" Kenya yelled over the music.

"What?" Whitney exclaimed.

"You were right…about Will. I confronted him, and he told me everything."

"I'm happy for you, Kenya. Glad you two worked it out."

"We didn't work it out." Kenya hung her head. "We broke up. The wedding's off."

Whitney looked at her friend for the first time. She sat on her couch, pain in her eyes and a look of defeat on her face. Tears welled in Kenya's eyes.

"I'm sorry, Kenya. I know how much this wedding meant to you."

Kenya cried. "He says he loves her." Her voice broke.

Whitney went over to the sofa, sat next to Kenya and wrapped her arms around her.

"I'm sorry, honey."

"I'm just glad I found out before we were married. Thank you for telling me. I know it must've been really hard for you, Whit."

"I didn't mean for it to come out like that. I wanted to do it another way."

"The truth is the truth, and I'm just glad we got down to it," said Kenya. "I must attract cheaters."

"No, honey, you don't attract cheaters. You're a good person and a great woman. Don't blame yourself for his horrible actions," said Whitney. "We shouldn't put so much merit into that damn Man Menu!"

"You're right. And I'm sorry about Lane. I wish I could take back every word we said on that phone."

"It's okay. I've moved on. It wasn't meant to be, obviously."

"When you were at dinner the other night, you said that you love him."

"What do I know? I don't even know what love is."

"You know when you love somebody, Whit. And I've never heard you use those words before."

"I was wrong." Whitney walked back over to the

piano. "I have a gig next weekend. At the lounge I was telling you about."

"He replied!" Kenya dried her tears and managed a smile.

"He said if he likes me, we could discuss a regular gig."

"How do you feel?"

"Nervous. But excited."

"You'll do fine, sister. And I'll be right there cheering you on."

"How's Tasha?"

"She's still mad, but she'll get over it. You know how she is. Just give her some time," said Kenya. "But we're good. You and me."

"We're good." Whitney stood and Kenya did, too. They embraced.

Chapter 26

When he read the message, he was instantly proud of her. Kenya had needed to make things right and managed to find Lane on Facebook. She sent him a message and invited him to Whitney's performance at a local lounge. She would be performing a few songs that she'd written, and she thought it would be an opportune time to get the lovebirds back together.

He smiled after he read the message, because he knew how badly Whitney had wanted this. She loved teaching school, but music was her passion. He sighed when he thought of her. She would be nervous, but she would do good. If he were still a part of her life, he would tell her to relax and just be herself. Since he wasn't in her life anymore, he thanked Kenya for the invitation but declined. She messaged back and left the address, just in case he changed his mind.

He shut his computer down and tossed it aside. Picked up the remote and looked for a game on television. He'd had a long tiring day, and all he wanted to do was relax and unwind. Besides, the invitation hadn't come from Whitney. Who was to say she even wanted him there. In fact, he hadn't heard from her since the night she walked out of his home. He'd reached out a couple of times, but she hadn't replied. He translated that as noninterest. However, he wanted her to be happy. Maybe she would meet someone who was more on her level—because according to her friends, he wasn't.

He glanced at the clock. It was a few minutes after eight. Part of him wanted to be there. If he dressed quickly, he could make it to the club by nine. Perhaps he'd just creep in and sit in the back. She wouldn't even have to know he was there. Even if she didn't know he was there, he would know in his heart that he had been there to support her.

He pulled himself up from the sofa, hopped into the shower. Slipped on a pair of slacks and a short-sleeved silk shirt. He dabbed some cologne onto his neck and placed a silver bracelet around his wrist. He brushed his hair, popped a mint into his mouth and headed out the door.

He stepped into the dark lounge, paid the cover charge and took a seat at a table in the back. Whitney was seated at the piano at the front of the room. She wore a white suit, with a black tight-fitting blouse underneath, the one he loved so much. She looked beautiful and he couldn't help staring. She seemed nervous and he wished he'd had an opportunity to give her that pep talk that she needed. She was a woman who didn't know her own capabilities. She doubted herself too much, in his opinion. She was an amazing woman and didn't even know it. He missed her. His heart ached.

The waitress in a short skirt brought him a vodka

and cranberry. He thanked her and gave her a smile. He listened as Whitney played and sang. The crowd was cooperative and shouted in agreement with her words. She sang about love and pain, and she was passionate about it. She sounded as if her heart had been broken. Lane took a sip of his drink as a wave of guilt passed through him.

When her set was over, he finished his drink and placed a twenty-dollar bill onto the table. He looked up and saw a woman watching him. He recognized her from her Facebook profile—Whitney's friend Kenya. Their eyes met and she smiled. He gave her a smile, stood and slipped out the door.

He unlocked his car, hopped in and turned the music up as he drove out of the parking lot. As much as he'd tried to erase his feelings for Whitney, he knew they were still there. However, he tucked them away and drove home. He had work on Saturday morning.

Chapter 27

Whitney felt good about her performance. It started off a bit rocky, but she'd managed to get a standing ovation at the end. She was so grateful for the audience participation when she sang the piece that she'd written just days before. It was a song about her breakup with Lane and the heartache she felt. She'd saved that one for last. Singing it was effortless; she just put her heart and soul into it.

Kenya was yelling as if they were at a Texas A&M football game. She smiled at her friend and shook her head. When she left the stage, she took a seat at the table next to her.

"You were so good, Whit! I was really feeling that song," she said. "It made me cry. I thought about Will."

"Aww, sweetie. I didn't mean to make you cry."

"It's okay. Maybe if I get it all out, I can stop crying so much."

Whitney's heart went out to her best friend. "We'll get through it together."

"At least your guy still loves you," she said.

"I doubt that." She raised her hand to get the waitress's attention.

"No, he really does."

The waitress appeared and gave Whitney a smile. "You really did a great job, girl," said the waitress.

"Thank you, sweetheart. I'll just have a rum and pineapple."

"Yes, ma'am. Right away."

"Lane was here," said Kenya after the waitress walked away.

"What are you talking about?"

"Don't be mad, but…" Kenya smiled sheepishly.

"But what? What did you do?"

"I reached out to him on Facebook. Told him about your performance tonight," she said. "And he came!"

"Right."

"He did! Sat right over there at that table." She pointed across the room. "He slipped out after your performance."

Whitney's heart beat rapidly. "Who cares? He didn't care enough to stick around."

"But he came, Whit. He loves you."

The waitress placed the cocktail on the table. "Here you go, Miss Talbot. Let me know if I can get you anything else."

Whitney gave her a smile. She changed the subject. "I think I might have a regular gig."

"I think so, honey. You rocked the house tonight," said Kenya.

"I did, didn't I?" Whitney giggled and took a sip of her cocktail.

* * *

She walked into her home, kicked her shoes off at the door. It had been a great night. Sean had asked if she could play again next Friday night, and she was elated. She had a week to work on some new material. She removed each piece of clothing as she made her way to her bedroom. She turned on the shower and hopped in. Tonight had been a great night.

Saturday morning came quickly. She rushed to meet Kenya at one of their favorite brunch spots. She walked to the table and to her surprise, Tasha was there, sipping on a glass of orange juice. Whitney was inclined to walk out but decided not to. She would face whatever Tasha had to offer.

"Hello," said Whitney.

"Hey, Whit," said Tasha. "Let's hash this out. We've been friends too long."

"I wasn't trying to hurt you," said Whitney. "Well, maybe I was. Because I was hurting, too. The two of you said some pretty mean things about Lane, and he heard every word."

"I'm sorry about that. I shouldn't have been so judgmental."

"Yes, you were." Whitney took a seat and signaled for the server.

"Aren't you sorry for what you said about Louis?"

"I didn't say anything that wasn't true. Louis *has* fathered a child since you've been together," said Whitney. "The point I was making was that the Man Menu is ridiculous. If you get all these wonderful qualities in a man but love and trust are not on the list, then what's the point? Seems worthless if you end up being disrespected in the end."

"We're working through our differences."

"That's great, and none of my business. I'm happy for you, whether you stay with Louis or leave him in the gutter," said Whitney. "I just wanted you to be happy. And I want you to be happy for me and whatever I decide."

"I realize now that I misjudged. And I would like to meet Lane."

"It's too late now. We broke up," Whitney said matter-of-factly and then turned to the server, who was standing there. "I'll start with a mimosa, and I'll have the chicken and waffles. Please bring a glass of water also."

"Will do, ma'am," said the blond-haired youngster as he disappeared.

"You broke up because of this?" Tasha asked.

"Because it just wasn't meant to be."

"I'm sorry, Whitney. The things I said that night were mean and uncalled for."

"It's okay. Really," said Whitney. "I'm sorry for attacking you about Louis."

"Water under the bridge." Tasha smiled. "I love you, sister."

"I love you back."

"Aww!" Kenya reached for Tasha's and Whitney's hands. The three of them held hands and raised them in the air. Their way of making things right between them.

"Whit, I know you weren't really interested before because you were involved with Lane, but Jason is still very interested in you," said Kenya.

"I know. He's been calling, but I haven't had a chance to call him back."

"I'm having a few friends over next Saturday for a barbecue, and I'd like for you to come. Jason will be there."

"I thought he was Will's friend," said Whitney.

"He's a mutual friend. I knew him first. And he was not happy with Will and how things turned out with us," said Kenya. "It's just a few people from the office coming, but I could really use my girls there as a distraction."

"Should I make my famous potato salad?" asked Tasha.

"Absolutely! The one that you pick up from the Kroger deli and pass off as yours?" Kenya giggled.

"Yes, that one." Tasha laughed.

"What about you, Whit? Can you bring something sweet?"

Whitney wasn't quite ready to socialize, and certainly not to date. Nothing about Jason interested her. "I can't. I…have…um…absolutely nothing to do, but I'm really not up for a bunch of people."

"Oh, come on, Whit," said Kenya.

"Ugh!" Whitney groaned. "Sure. I'll grab some cupcakes from my favorite bakery. And I'll make some Bahamian macaroni and cheese."

"Yay!" Kenya and Tasha both sang, and clapped.

Maybe it was time she met some new people. What harm could it do?

Chapter 28

Cars were parked along the block and in Kenya's driveway. Whitney could hear laughter and chatter in the air as she made her way to the backyard, a pan of mac and cheese and red velvet cupcakes in her hands. Kenya's brother was flipping burgers on the grill. Tasha was seated under the gazebo chattering with a group of ladies. Kenya came out of the back door carrying a plate filled with steaks and hot dogs. She spotted Whitney and smiled. Whitney followed her to the grill.

"Hey, Trey," she said to Kenya's brother.

"Whitney, you're looking good," said Trey. "Still single?"

"I think I will be forever." Whitney laughed.

"Well, remember our deal. If we're both still single in ten years, we marry each other," said Trey. "Don't forget."

"I remember."

The two of them shook hands and laughed.

"You two need to stop," said Kenya as she handed Trey the platter of meat for the grill. She grabbed the cupcakes from Whitney and then grabbed her by the arm. "Come on, girl, let's go inside."

"Take care of that body, babe," said Trey. "Stay fit for me."

Whitney laughed at Trey. She'd always thought he'd missed his calling. He should've been a comedian. "Okay, sweetie, I'll do my best."

"Please don't entertain him."

"I have to." Whitney laughed.

They walked into Kenya's massive kitchen, with dark wooden cabinets and large island, granite counters, and silver appliances. Whitney placed the macaroni and cheese onto the island with the rest of the sides—potato salad, deviled eggs, fruit and baked beans. Whitney grabbed a wineglass from the cabinet and poured herself a glass. Soft music played in the house, something soulful.

"Hey, hey, hey! Is anybody home?" someone called out. A tall, dark and very attractive man walked into the kitchen.

"Jason!" said Kenya. "You made it!"

He walked over and kissed Kenya's cheek. "I told you I would."

"Yes, you did."

He glanced at Whitney and their eyes locked.

"Hello," he said.

"Jason, that is my friend Whitney. I believe you've spoken with her on the phone a time or two. Whitney, Jason."

"Ahh, the woman who blew me off." He grinned a beautiful grin. "Pleasure to finally meet you."

"You, too," said Whitney and shook his strong hand. "And I didn't blow you off."

"What would you call it?" he asked and then popped a deviled egg into his mouth.

"It was just a bad time."

"I see," said Jason. "I forgive you."

"Thank you." Whitney met his beautiful white smile with hers.

"I'm going to check on those steaks," said Kenya. "If I don't watch Trey, he'll burn them."

She was alone with Jason and his piercing eyes. He wore a gray polo that hugged his biceps, jeans and gray leather loafers. She had to admit, he was pleasant to look at. They chitchatted in the kitchen for a bit. He spent a great deal of time talking about his business, which he'd started right out of college, and the real estate that he owned throughout the state of Texas. He was quite proud of those things. She didn't have a chance to brag on her children or tell him about her musical endeavors.

"Do you think I can take you out to dinner?" he finally asked.

"Sure, I don't think that will be a problem."

"How about tomorrow we do a Sunday matinee and dinner afterward? If you're free."

"I think I'm free."

"Fantastic." He smiled. "I'm going to grab one of those steaks off the grill. I like mine medium, and I want to catch one before it's too done."

"Okay." Whitney stood there for a moment and sipped her wine.

As the sun began to set, she sat under the gazebo laughing and talking to Kenya, Tasha and a few other women who had attended the barbecue. Jason had long gone, but she was looking forward to their date on Sunday. She needed a distraction from her thoughts of Lane. He was there, in her mind, all the time. She couldn't rid her thoughts of him. A date with someone else might just do the trick.

She did everything in her power not to fall asleep during the movie. It wasn't one that she'd have gone to see. She enjoyed comedies and love stories. Sci-fi wasn't really her genre of choice, but she was a compromiser. She was counting down the moments until it ended. She was anxious to get to dinner, because her stomach was growling. She hoped he hadn't heard it.

Finally, she sat in front of him, a menu in her hands. She gave it a quick glance and decided on something suitable. She longed for an order of those hot wings that she usually got from the sports bar that she and Lane had frequented. She wished she were at a place where she didn't have to be cognizant of her elbows being on the table or have to decide which fork she should use. She and Lane usually enjoyed places where they ate with their fingers and sipped on beers.

"Have you decided on something?"

"Yes, I think I'll have a juicy burger," she stated.

"Really? This place boasts their prime steaks—filets, sirloins and rib eyes. And you'd rather have a juicy burger?"

"That's my mood right now, yes."

Jason chuckled. "Whatever the lady wants."

When the server approached the table, he smiled broadly. "Good afternoon, Mr. Fisch. What can I get for you and the lady this evening?"

"Charlés, I'll have the filet, medium, with the garlic

mashed potatoes and a double portion of vegetables."
Jason chuckled. "And for the lady…sadly, she wants
the burger…"

"How would you like that cooked, ma'am?" Charles
asked.

"Medium well." Whitney gave Charles a smile.

"And, Charles, bring her the petit sirloin, as well.
There's no way I'll allow her to leave here without trying one of your delectable steaks," said Jason, "and
please bring your best bottle of Cabernet Sauvignon."

Allow her? Those words stuck with her long after
Charles had disappeared. *And who wants to eat a juicy
burger and a petit sirloin?* The first time that Lane ordered for her, she'd thought it was cute. She smiled at
the thought. This? Not so much. She would get through
the night, but there wouldn't be a second date.

When he walked her to the door, he pulled her in for
a hug. He kissed her cheek.

"I'd love to come in and chat for a bit," he whispered.

"You know," she started, "it's a school night, and I
have a very early morning."

"I understand." He smiled. "I have an early morning also. Maybe we can get together later in the week."

"Maybe." She smiled and turned to unlock her door.

"I'll call you," he said.

"You do that."

She exhaled when she was on the other side of her
door. She heard the engine from his overpriced sports
car fire up. She kicked her shoes off and peeled her
clothes from her tired body. She started the shower and
then changed her mind. This was a more of a bubble-
bath night.

Chapter 29

He missed her like he missed his mother's collard greens. He missed her conversation, her smile and laughter. He missed her body and the way she made him feel. She was beautiful and sexy, and she knew him better than anyone. And it was ridiculous that they weren't together. Each of them too stubborn to give in to the other. Somebody had to call a truce, and he guessed it should be him.

It was Sunday night and he knew he had an early morning. So did she, for that matter. But he didn't care. He needed her back in his life. This nonsense had gone on long enough. He hopped into his truck, stopped at Kroger and picked up a bouquet of roses and drove to her house. If he called her, she might not pick up. But if he showed up on her doorstep, she might be forced to hear him out as he begged for her forgiveness.

When he pulled up in front of her house, his intent was to apologize profusely. However, he was surprised to learn that she'd moved on so quickly. He watched as some suit-and-tie walked her to her front door and kissed her good-night.

He had pulled into her subdivision and crept down her block. Just as he reached her house, he saw them. She and some other dude pulled up in a fancy sports car. He didn't even have the decency to open her door, just stood at the front of the car and waited for her to get out. The two of them made their way to the front door. They chatted for a bit and then he kissed her cheek. This was definitely a date, Lane thought. She'd already been on a date, as if what they had didn't even matter. He watched as Whitney went inside and Mr. Nerdy Ass drove away in his expensive Tesla coupe.

He was jealous. He was convinced that he had been right all along, and so had her friends—that he wasn't what she was looking for. He peeled out of her subdivision and headed for Max's and dialed Melvin's phone number. He needed a drink before he turned in for the night.

"Meet me at Max's for a drink."

"Can't, bro. Work early in the morning."

"When has that ever stopped you from drinking with your brother?"

"It's not a good time."

"What is it I'm hearing in your voice?"

"What are you talking about?"

"Something's different. Haven't seen or heard from you in a couple of weeks, and now you're turning down Max's. What's going on?"

"You could've let me know that you let Tyler go."

"I didn't let Tyler go. The company did."

"But you didn't fight for him," accused Melvin.

"Excuse me? I got suspended because I refused to fire Tyler."

"Yet he still got fired. He lost his car, and now he might get evicted from his new apartment, bro."

"Hey, you asked me to give him a chance and I did. I can't control what happened after that," said Lane. "And for your information, I did fight for him. Put my own job on the line."

"It's cool, man."

"Are you done?"

"Yeah, I'm done."

"Good!" Lane hung up the phone. The nerve of him.

He took a seat at the bar and ordered a Heineken with a lime. He glanced at the television mounted over the bar. The Mavs were winning, but he didn't care one way or the other. His night had been filled with a myriad of emotions. Seemed endless. He wanted to punch something, but instead he slammed his beer and then ordered another. He needed to calm down.

"Bad night?" Max took a seat next to him. The men shook hands.

"You can say that."

"Let's take a walk."

Lane followed Max to his small office in the back. Max moved files and boxes out of the chair on the opposite side of his desk.

"Have a seat, man," he offered. "Excuse the mess. I need to get this place cleaned up."

Lane took a seat.

"Thanks."

"What's going on?" asked Max.

"This woman…" Lane sighed.

"The Caribbean one," said Max. "You went back and made amends, right?"

"I went over there tonight to do just that, and she was just coming home from a date with another guy. I think I've lost her for good."

"Didn't you say that she loves you?"

"I can't compete with this guy." Lane crossed his legs. "He drives a damn Tesla."

Max laughed. "And you think that she's moved on that quickly?"

"I think so." Lane shrugged his shoulders.

"I wouldn't give up on her," said Max. "Unless she's a gold digger, she doesn't care that the guy has money or that he drives a Tesla."

"She and her girlfriends have this Man Menu. It's like the guys they date have to meet all this criteria. I'm sure I didn't measure up."

"Don't be so hard on yourself, bro. You're a great catch. You have a great job, your own home. Good-looking. Not quite as good-looking as me." Max laughed. "But you're a great catch. I'm sure she knows that, and if she doesn't...well, so be it. There are other fish in the sea."

"That's the thing, man. I only want that fish."

"I hear you, man. We want what we want, don't we?"

"We want what we want," Lane repeated and reclined in the chair. "Then there's this thing with Melvin. His nephew was getting into some trouble back home in Saint Louis, and when he moved here, Melvin asked if I could get him on at the company. I did it as a favor to my buddy. But then his past came back to haunt him. He was tardy one too many times, and I was asked to fire him."

"Oh, wow."

"I refused and ended up suspended because of it."

"Damn, sounds like you put your ass on the line for a friend."

"Damn right I did! But I just got off the phone with Melvin, and he's all up in arms because Tyler still ended up fired, even after I'd gone to bat for him."

"That's not your fault," said Max.

"That's what I said!"

"I wouldn't stress too much over Melvin. He'll come around. You guys have been friends way too long. And he'll see that he's wrong on this one."

"Nonetheless, it's been a hell of a night."

"I'll say."

"But it's been cool talking it out with you, man. Thanks," said Lane. "I needed to vent."

"Anytime," said Max. "By the way, I've decided not to sell the bar."

"You and the wife are working things out?"

"No, but I'm hoping to get a loan to keep things going," said Max. "The fellow who owns the place is still waiting for me to lose it. Wants to turn it into a gentlemen's club. An upscale one."

"Can't let that happen, can we?"

"Nah. That's not what Max's is. It's a family place. Down-to-earth. A place where people from all walks of life can come and let their hair down."

"It's definitely been that place for me," said Lane. "I have to say that I'm a bit relieved. I wasn't quite ready to buy the place outright. I wouldn't know the first thing about running a bar. I just thought that I needed to be a business owner to impress some people."

"Everybody's not cut out for this. It's a lot of work," said Max. "But it's what I know."

"And you're great at it."

"I need help, though," said Max. "Maybe we can talk about a partnership instead."

"I could probably handle that," said Lane. "I can probably invest the money that you need to keep the doors open. Maybe I can be a silent partner."

"Let's see how things go at the bank, and we'll talk about it."

"Sounds like a plan." Lane shook Max's hand.

Max stood. "How about another drink?"

"Nah. I'd better turn in for the night. Mornings come a lot faster than expected." Lane followed Max out of his office and to the door of the bar. "I'm going to call it a night."

"Don't put too much worry into things, man. Give yourself a few days, and things will work out. Melvin will come around. And as for the woman you love, if it's meant to be…"

"Yeah, I know. If it's meant to be, it will be."

"Exactly!"

The two shook hands, and Lane walked out into the night. He drove home, his radio tuned to the Dallas radio station, 105.7. He cracked the window a bit and rested his head against the seat as he drove home.

Chapter 30

She didn't know what made her agree to a weekend getaway with Jason, to his home on Galveston Island. Her mind said a resounding *no* when he asked, but her mouth defied her and said *yes* instead. On their first date, he'd spent more time talking about himself and handling business on his phone than getting to know her. She'd never felt more alone while in the company of another person. He was nothing like Lane, and she missed him dearly. But she justified it by telling herself that Jason was a nice distraction while trying with all her might to get Lane out of her system. Jason didn't have all of the qualities she was looking for, but he had a good percentage. And he was anxious to show her just how much he had to offer.

At least he'd gained Tasha's approval, which was unusual. And she had everything he was looking for, too. She was a nice trophy for his arm, and he'd planned to show her off when he entertained his colleagues. When Jason invited Whitney to his beach home in Galveston for the weekend, he presented it as a way for them to get away and become better acquainted. However, the first night of their weekend he was planning a huge party for his colleagues. He literally said that her only job was to smile and be beautiful.

When they arrived, she was in awe of the beauty of the place. There were mahogany wood floors throughout, silver appliances, French doors off the formal living room and hundreds of windows everywhere. The view of the ocean was breathtaking, and the home had been professionally decorated.

"I'll just place your things in here," he said after giving her a quick tour. "This is the master. I'm sure you'll be quite comfortable."

"I'm sure I will." She stepped into the master bedroom and took a look around. It was beautiful. A huge king-size bed was in the center of the room, with huge posts and a canopy, with large matching dressers. A tasteful portrait hung over the bed.

There was a dress laid out on the bed.

"I'd like for you to wear that tonight, if you don't mind," said Jason.

"I actually packed a nice dress," she said.

"If you don't mind," he insisted. "I'll leave you to unwind and get settled. I have to run out for a bit, but the guests will begin to arrive about eight. If you could be ready before then, that would be great."

Before she could protest or inquire about any other details, he was gone. She heard the engine from his SUV fire up and he'd already pulled out of the circular drive. She was alone, and part of her felt grateful. She flipped on the television that was hidden inside a credenza. Found the channel for the NCAA basketball tournament. Lane's alma mater, Missouri State University, was playing during college basketball's March Madness. She wondered if he was watching. In fact, she knew he was watching. She hoped they would win.

She went down the hallway and into the kitchen in search of a beverage. There wasn't much in the refrigerator, as Jason was probably shopping for groceries. She didn't know how often he frequented the home. She found a beer in the fridge but wasn't quite sure how long it had been there. She wasn't much of a beer drinker, but she needed one today. She searched the kitchen drawers for a bottle opener. Once she'd found it, she popped the top off her beer and took a drink. Went back into the bedroom, kicked her shoes off, hopped onto the bed and watched the game. She cheered for Lane's team.

The closer it got to eight o'clock, the more she regretted her decision to accompany him on this trip. But she reluctantly hopped into the shower, rubbed lotion all over her body and slipped into the skimpy dress that Jason had chosen for her to wear. She would get through the night and tomorrow she'd be back in Dallas in her comfortable home. And she was definitely taking a walk along that ocean before the night was over. Texas beaches were nothing like the ones in the Bahamas, but it was an ocean nonetheless.

Soon the house was filled with strangers—Jason's friends and colleagues, people she'd never met before in her life. Jason got lost in the crowd as she attempted to make small talk with some of his friends. They had nothing in common with her, and she quickly became bored.

She slipped out the side door and decided to retreat to the beach. She removed her heels and her feet touched the warm sand. She looked up at the stars in the dark sky and smiled. She watched as the water brushed against the shore. The tide wasn't high. In fact, it was quite calm. She let the water touch her feet. The ocean always made her feel better. However, thoughts of Lane consumed her. She missed him desperately. Wondered what he was doing. He usually worked most Saturdays and found himself retired to the sofa for the night. He was probably flipping the channels back and forth between basketball games and deciding which team he'd place his bet on. She giggled at the thought. He was an undercover gambler and in denial. She didn't care. She loved him despite his vices.

After she had a good stroll, she returned to the house.

"Where have you been? I've been looking for you," said Jason.

"I went for a stroll on the beach."

"I was worried." He lowered his voice to a whisper so that his guests couldn't hear his reprimand.

She couldn't believe that she was being reprimanded by a guy she barely knew. She retreated to the kitchen, poured herself a glass of wine and nibbled on chunks of cheese, summer sausage and fruit slices. She hopped onto one of the bar stools at the island with the granite top. She was lonely and bored but was relieved when she finally heard people saying their goodbyes and beginning to leave.

After most guests were gone except for a few, she made her way back to the master bedroom. She thought it appropriate to shut the door, take herself a long bubble bath and change into a pair of sweats and a T-shirt. It was time to unwind. It wasn't like anyone would be looking for her. She decided to find a late-night movie and watch until her eyelids could no longer stay open.

Jason and the few guests that were left spent a few hours chatting.

After everyone was bid a farewell, a drunken Jason burst into the master bedroom and collapsed onto the bed. She'd misunderstood. She hadn't thought he'd be sleeping in the room with her. After all, there were plenty of other bedrooms and she told him so.

"Did you think we weren't going to sleep together?" he asked as he removed his trousers, down to his boxer shorts.

She was stunned. "This is not what I came here for."

"Well, what did you come here for? What were you thinking this was?"

"I'd like to go home, please."

"Are you crazy? Dallas is not around the corner."

She stood and he stood, too, blocked the door. She tried to reach around him for the handle and he became aggressive, grabbed her. He grabbed a handful of her breast and smiled. She backed away, but he reached for her, held on to her tightly. She tried with all her might to free herself from his grasp, but he was much stronger. She tussled with him a bit, and when she kneed him in the groin, he quickly understood the meaning of the word *no*.

She grabbed her cell phone from the bed, rushed past him, swung the bedroom door open and took off running right out the front door. She escaped to the beach where she'd gone before. She unlocked her cell phone but had no idea who she would call. She would have called one of her brothers to rescue her had they been closer. However, her brother Edward was in Florida, Nate in Atlanta, and her youngest brother, Denny, was the farthest away, in the Bahamas. She'd have called Kenya, but she knew that Kenya didn't drive long distances alone, and she would worry herself silly all night until she knew that Whitney was safe. She considered calling Kenya's brother, Trey, but didn't have his phone number in her phone.

She thought of Lane. Contemplated calling him, but how would she explain where she was and why? Would he even pick up? He probably hated her at the moment, and she'd feel like crap if he blew her off. However, she really needed him. She didn't have anyone else. She dialed his number. She didn't expect him to pick up, but he picked up on the second ring.

"Hello, stranger," he said. His voice sounded so good and so cheerful. Not a bit of hate in it.

She began to cry.

"Whitney?" he said.

"I need you." She managed to get those words out.

"What's wrong, baby?" he asked. So much concern in his voice. And it felt so good to hear him call her *baby*.

"I'm in a situation," she said and explained what was happening.

He didn't hesitate to say "I'm coming to get you right now!"

Relief overtook her body as she hung up.

She quietly paced along the shores of the Gulf of Mexico as she patiently awaited Lane's arrival. There were people on the beach, even as late as it was. Lovers cuddled on beach towels along the shore. She glanced at the house and could see Jason pacing back and forth through the glass windows. He didn't look concerned enough to come look for her, and she was grateful. Soon she didn't see him pacing anymore and assumed he'd passed out in a drunken sleep.

In the matter of four hours that it took for Lane to

travel from Dallas to Galveston, Whitney had made her way back to the house and taken a seat on the front steps. She saw the lights from Lane's truck as he drove slowly down the block. She recognized his truck as soon as he turned onto the street. Her heart pounded. She was grateful to be leaving, but even more grateful that she'd be seeing his beautiful face in just a matter of minutes. She'd missed him so. He pulled into the circular drive and hopped out of the truck. She stood.

"Hey," he said when he saw her.

She didn't say anything, just rushed to him quickly and collapsed into his arms. Her hero had come to her rescue. He kissed her lips and held her tightly. She didn't want him to let her go.

"I'm so glad you're here," she whispered.

"Are you okay?" he asked.

"I am now."

He took her by the hand and walked her toward the truck. "Do you need to get your things?"

"I'll get them another time."

"You sure? Because I'll make him give you your things," said Lane.

"There's nothing in there that can't be replaced."

"Ready, then?"

She shook her head yes.

Lane opened the passenger's door of his Ford F-150, and she hopped inside. He got inside and started the engine. When she heard Lil Wayne's voice fill the truck's cab, she smiled. She was home.

She looked over at him. Couldn't stop staring. "Thank you," she said.

He looked at her. Smiled. "What were you doing with that creep, anyway?"

"Trying to forget about you," she admitted. "I missed you."

"I missed you, too." He leaned over and kissed her. "I know that I don't have everything that you're looking for..."

"You have everything that I need."

"I know your friends don't think I'm good enough for you."

"I don't care what they think. I know what I want."

He looked over at her. She wanted him so bad at that moment. She knew that he was not a perfect man, but she couldn't help thinking that he was perfect for her.

Chapter 31

He held her close to his heart, because that's where she belonged. That was where she would stay. He wouldn't allow her out of his grasp again.

"Are you sleeping?"

"No," she said softly. "Listening to your heartbeat."

"I thought I'd lost you for good. I saw you with *him* the other night."

"Him who?" she asked, and leaned her head up and placed her chin on his chest.

"I think you know." He smiled knowingly.

"Were you stalking me?"

"No, I came to your house that night to apologize and make things right. But you were with *him*. I saw him walk you to the door, kiss you on the cheek."

"Wow! And you didn't say anything?"

"Kinda like you did when you saw me with Nicole."

"Touché," said Whitney. "It meant nothing, though. The entire time I was with him, I was thinking of you."

"That sounds like such a line." He laughed.

"It's the truth." She laughed, too. "I swear."

"It's the truth, I swear," he mocked her and then pulled her into him, kissed her.

His tongue danced inside her mouth as she lay on top of his chest. He massaged the roundness of her backside. His fingertips danced up and down her side and then caressed her breasts. He grabbed one in his palms and wrapped his lips around it. Whitney moaned. He'd missed the sounds that she made when he pleased her.

He rolled over and placed her beneath him, hovered over her. Kissed the space between her breasts. His lips then trailed her stomach and danced around her belly button. He kissed his way down to her thighs and lingered on the inside of them. His tongue began to dance in her sweet spot. She moaned again and gave him adventurousness to continue. Her legs trembled and her belly followed. He'd attained his goal of bringing her to climax. She breathed heavily and then he quickly moved up and placed himself inside her.

"I love you," she whispered.

"I love you, too," he whispered back and showed her just how much.

She wrapped her brown legs around his waist, and before long he grasped her tightly as he reached his peak. He groaned with desire and then collapsed on top of her.

The smell of bacon brushed across his nose and he struggled to open his eyes. He looked over at the empty space next to him in bed. He pulled himself out of bed, went into the bathroom, brushed his teeth and washed his face. Crept into the kitchen. Whitney was standing in front of the stove wearing a T-shirt and a pair of boy-cut shorts. She swung her hips to the Rihanna tune that played softly on the stereo. She didn't hear him enter the room and he liked it that way. He loved watching her. He leaned against the wall with his arms folded across his chest and enjoyed the view.

She turned around and caught him spying. A smile spread across her face.

"There you go with those stalker moves again," she said.

"I'm not stalking. I'm admiring."

She walked over and wrapped her arms around his waist, kissed his lips. "Did you sleep well?"

"Yes, I did."

She walked back over to the stove and he followed. "I could tell, the way you were snoring."

He stole a piece of bacon. "I don't snore."

"Who told you that lie?" she asked. "As my dad would say, you were calling the hogs."

"Right!" He snatched another piece of bacon and she slapped his hand. He slapped her on the behind. "I'm going to get dressed. I have a run to make."

"Where are you going?" she asked with a smirk.

"Can't tell you."

"To place a bet?" she yelled as he left the room. She knew him too well.

He pulled into the parking lot and stepped inside the door. The jeweler recognized him immediately. He remembered how extremely specific he'd been about what he wanted. He wanted the elegant round ruby—her birthstone—with two glittering white diamond accents on each side. And he'd had it engraved with their names.

"I didn't think you were coming back for it," said

the jeweler. "You paid in full but never returned to pick it up.

"I wasn't sure if things were going to work out," said Lane.

"But you're sure now?" asked the jeweler.

"I'm pretty sure. I'm not letting her go this time."

The jeweler smiled. "Let me package it for you, sir."

"Thank you."

She'd already eaten by the time he returned.

"I tried to wait for you," she said as she sat at his kitchen table.

"It's okay, babe." He took a seat next to hers. Grabbed her hand, stared into her eyes.

"What is wrong with you?" she asked with a giggle, and stuffed eggs into her mouth.

He reached into the pocket of his jeans and pulled out the black velvet ring box. He opened it and held it in front of her face.

She gasped.

"It's not an engagement ring." He grinned. "It's a promise ring. I promise that I'll always be here for you whenever you need me. I won't ever abandon you again. I promise to love you until we make the decision to love each other for life."

"Really? Wow. It's beautiful. And my birthstone." She admired the ring. "It looks custom."

"It is. It's engraved, too."

She read the engraving. *Whitney and Lane for now.*

"For now?" she asked.

"For now, until we get to *forever*."

"That's sweet." She leaned over and kissed him.

He took the ring from her fingertips. Placed it between his lips and slid the ring onto her left ring finger with his mouth. Her finger lingered in his mouth for a moment. Tears formed in her eyes.

"Don't cry, baby. This is a happy moment," he whispered.

"I am happy. I was so unhappy when you were gone. I don't ever want to be without you again."

"I'm not going anywhere."

She placed her hands on each side of his face. Her touch was gentle against his five-o'clock shadow. He reached over and brushed the tears from her eyes.

Chapter 32

She wore a sexy red dress. It hugged her hips seductively and the back was dangerously low. She pulled her hair into a bun on her head. Pearls were wrapped around her neck and the ruby ring sparkled every time she waved her hand. And she waved it a lot! She held on to Lane's arm. He looked dapper in his tailored gray suit and red tie.

"You're more lovely than he described," said Max after Lane introduced them.

"Thank you. It's wonderful to finally meet you, as well," said Whitney.

"Well, you'll be seeing a lot of me, now that this guy is my partner."

"Congratulations to you both!" She smiled. "I'm quite proud."

"Thank you, baby." Lanc kissed her cheek.

"I think I see Kenya over there. I'm going to run over and say hello." She excused herself.

As she walked away, she had a feeling that Lane was watching the swing of her hips. She turned around. He was, in fact, watching. When she caught him, he winked his eye at her. She blushed and then gave him a seductive smile. There was no denying she loved that man.

"Well, well, well," said Kenya.

"Well what?"

"You and Lane found each other again, I see."

"Yes, we did."

Kenya had no idea how she and Lane had reconnected. Whitney hadn't shared the details of what happened with Jason, and obviously he hadn't either. She hadn't heard from him after that night, and she was fine with that. She didn't care if she never heard from him again.

"Honey, you are glowing!" said Kenya.

"I am, aren't I?"

"And you're blinging, too!" Kenya grabbed Whitney's left hand and observed the ring. "What's this? Did you forget to tell me something?"

"It's a promise ring," said Whitney. "He promised he would never abandon me again."

"Aww! That's sweet," said Kenya. "Didn't discuss marriage?"

"No. Neither of us is ready for that."

"That's good. Take your time. Don't run into anything too soon like I did."

"Have you talked to him?" Whitney asked.

"Not since that day," said Kenya. "But I'm happy that Max decided not to sell the place. And I'm glad that he didn't lose it to Will."

"Me, too. I'm happy for Lane. He's now a business owner."

"You know what that means, right?" asked Kenya. "He meets another criteria on your Man Menu."

"I don't care about that stupid Man Menu," said Whitney. "I don't care if he doesn't meet anything on it. I love him endlessly."

"I'm so happy for you, Whit. You finally found love."

"I finally did." Whitney rested her head on Kenya's shoulder.

"What's this about love?" asked Tasha as she walked up.

"Our girl is in love," Kenya explained. "She found the real thing."

"Really?" Tasha asked skeptically. "I hope he doesn't disappoint."

"He won't!" said a confident Whitney.

"Well, I'm happy for you." Tasha grabbed Whitney's hand.

"And, darling, did you see the ring?" Kenya grinned like a proud parent. "That boy has taste."

"Yes, he does," said Tasha as she observed the ruby. "Is this what I think it is?"

"It's a promise ring. We're taking it slow."

"Well, if he makes promises with rubies, what will he do for lifetime commitments, honey?" asked Tasha.

"I don't know, but I'm looking forward to finding out."

"Looks like he might be a keeper, sweetie." Tasha gave Whitney a strong, genuine hug. "I'm gonna go work the room."

Lane approached Whitney and Kenya. He handed Whitney a glass of Riesling and gave Kenya a smile. "Thank you for coming, Kenya."

"I wouldn't have missed it for the world. Congratulations to you!"

"Thanks!"

The three of them chatted for a moment. Lane's best friend, Melvin, walked up and patted Lane on the back.

"Good evening, ladies," said Melvin.

"Hello," said both Whitney and Kenya in harmony.

"Hey, brother," he said to Lane. "How are you?"

Lane's face was hard. He didn't crack a smile and didn't seem happy to see his friend.

"I'm good. What are you doing here?"

Whitney's and Kenya's eyes met in confusion. She pretended to observe the crowd. Max's was filled with people there to celebrate the men's new venture.

"I'm going over here to see what Tasha's up to," Kenya excused herself and then disappeared into the crowd.

"I heard about your partnership with Max. Wanted to come by and say congratulations," said Melvin.

"Thanks," said Lane unenthusiastically.

Whitney was confused by Lane's indifference toward his best friend.

"Can I talk to you for a moment?" Melvin asked Lane. "In private."

"Anything you need to say can be said in front of my woman. We have no secrets."

Obviously they did have secrets, because she hadn't a clue about what was going on. She felt a bit of discomfort, but she was curious to know what had transpired with Lane and his friend of many years. He hadn't shared anything with her. She stood there.

"I'm sorry about the way I came at you the other day. I was completely out of line."

"You absolutely were."

"I'm thankful that you even gave Tyler a chance. And that you stuck your neck out for him."

Lane just bobbed his head in agreement.

"Tyler caused his own problems, and he'll find another job soon. He just needs to get out there and look."

"Well, you'll be happy to know that I was able to get him his job back. I had a chat with the owner."

"Wow! Really, man?"

"I planned on giving him a call in the morning," said Lane.

"Do you mind if I tell him?"

"Not at all."

"Thanks again, man. You're really a true friend. And I've been an ass. I hope you can forgive me," said Melvin. "I'm going to go over and holler at Max."

"Tell the bartender to give you a Rémy on the rocks. Put it on my tab," said Lane. He shook hands with his friend and the men embraced.

Melvin headed toward the bar.

"And what was that all about?" asked Whitney.

"Old wounds," said Lane. "This night is about new beginnings. Come on, let me show you off."

The two worked the room, and Whitney felt very confident with Lane. He made her feel as if she was the most beautiful woman in the room. He held her hand in his and introduced her to several people. Eventually, her feet hurt and she took a seat at the bar and continued to watch him work the room. She glanced across the room and noticed that Melvin and Kenya had become quite cozy in a dark corner. She smiled. Her friend needed some fun in her life. Tasha was running her mouth with Max. Whitney knew that she was probably lecturing him about his financial portfolio and offering her services.

She looked at the ruby on her finger and then glanced across the room at the man who gave it to her. She was happy—truly happy.

* * *

At the end of the night, Lane drove them home. When he hopped onto Interstate 35, she reached into her purse and pulled out the typewritten copy of her Man Menu. She'd carried it folded in her purse since college. The paper was worn and somewhat falling apart. She gave it a quick glance and then ripped it to shreds, tossed it out the window and watched as the pieces blew in the wind. She looked at her imperfect man and gave him a smile. He was all the man she needed.

* * * * *

Check out the previous books in the
THE TALBOLTS OF HARBOR ISLAND *series*
by Monica Richardson:

AN ISLAND AFFAIR
A YULETIDE AFFAIR
SECOND CHANCE SEDUCTION

Available now from Harlequin Kimani Romance!

KIMANI™
ROMANCE

COMING NEXT MONTH
Available September 26, 2017

#541 NEVER CHRISTMAS WITHOUT YOU
by Nana Malone and Reese Ryan
This collection features two sizzling holiday stories from fan-favorite authors. Unwrap the ultimate gift of romance as two couples explore the magic of true love at Christmas.

#542 TEMPTED AT TWILIGHT
Tropical Destiny • **by Jamie Pope**
Nothing fires up trauma surgeon Elias Bradley like the risk of thrilling adventure. But when he meets Dr. Cricket Warren, she awakens emotions that take him by surprise. And now she's having his baby… He's ready to step up, but can they turn a fantasy into a lifetime of romance?

#543 THE HEAT BETWEEN US
Southern Loving • **by Cheris Hodges**
Appointed to head Atlanta's first-ever jazz festival, marketing guru Michael "MJ" Jane sets out to create an annual event to rival New Orleans. Even if that means hiring her crush and former marine Jamal Carver to run security. Can love keep Jamal and MJ in harmony…forever?

#544 SIZZLING DESIRE
Love on Fire • **by Kayla Perrin**
Lorraine Mitchell cannot forget her heated encounter with firefighter Hunter Holland. Weeks later, she is stunned to discover that his father—a former patient of hers—has left her a large bequest! Despite mutual mistrust, reviving their spark might ignite a love that's as deep as it is scorching…

Get 2 Free Books,
Plus 2 Free Gifts—
just for trying the Reader Service!

KIMANI™ ROMANCE

*Flirting with a gorgeous stranger at the bar is how
Lorraine Mitchell celebrates her longed-for newly single
status. One-night stands usually run hot and wild before
quickly flaming out, but Lorraine cannot forget her heated
encounter with firefighter Hunter Holland. And reviving
their spark just might ignite a love that's as deep and true
as it is scorching...*

*Read on for a sneak peek at
SIZZLING DESIRE,
the next exciting installment in author
Keyla Perrin's **LOVE ON FIRE** series!*

"You know why I'm here tonight," Lorraine said to Hunter
as they neared the bar. "What brings you here?"

"I'm new in town," Hunter explained.

"Aah. Are you new to California?" Lorraine asked. "Did
you move here from another state?"

"I did, yes. But I'm not new to Ocean City. I grew up
here, then moved to Reno when I hit eighteen. I lived and
worked there for sixteen years, and now I'm back. I'm a
firefighter."

That explained why he was in such good shape.
Firefighters were strong, their bodies immaculately honed
in order to be able to rescue people from burning buildings
and other disastrous situations. No wonder he had come to
her aid in such a chivalrous way.

She swayed a little—deliberately—so she could wrap her fingers tighter around his arm. Yes, she was shamelessly copping a feel. She barely even recognized herself.

"Oops," Hunter said, securing his hand on her back to make sure she was steady. "You okay?"

"I'm fine," Lorraine said. "You're so sweet." *And so hot.*

So hot that she wanted to smooth her hands over his muscular pecs for a few glorious minutes.

She turned away from him and continued toward the bar. What was going on with her? It must be the alcohol making her react so strongly to this man.

Though the truth was, she didn't care what was bringing out this reaction in her. Because every time Hunter looked at her, she felt incredibly desirable—something she hadn't felt with Paul since the early days of their marriage. But unlike her ex-husband, Hunter's attraction for her was obvious in that dark, intense gaze. Every time their eyes connected, the chemistry sizzled.

Lorraine's heart was pounding with excitement, and it was a wonderful feeling after all the pain and heartache she'd gone through recently. It was nice to feel the pitter-patter of her pulse because of a guy who rated eleven out of ten on the sexy scale.

Lorraine veered to the left to sidestep a group of women. And all of a sudden, her heel twisted beneath her body. This time, she started to go down in earnest. Hunter quickly swooped his arms around her, and the next thing she knew, he was scooping her into his arms.

"Oh, my God," she uttered. "You're not carrying me—"

Don't miss SIZZLING DESIRE
by Kayla Perrin, available October 2017
wherever Harlequin® Kimani Romance™
books and ebooks are sold!

KPEXP0917

LOVE
Harlequin
romance?

Join our Harlequin community to share your thoughts and connect with other romance readers!

Be the first to find out about promotions, news, and exclusive content!

Sign up for the Harlequin e-newsletter and download a free book from any series at

www.TryHarlequin.com

Want to give in to temptation with
steamy tales of irresistible desire?

Check out **Harlequin® Presents®,
Harlequin® Desire** and
Harlequin® Kimani™ Romance books!

New books available every month!

CONNECT WITH US AT:

Harlequin.com/Community

**ROMANCE WHEN
YOU NEED IT**

PGENRE2017